Nine on

AN arranged marriage falls tragic...
In a beauty parlour, friendly gossip ...... uncomfortable truths. In pre-independent India, a young widow fights to succeed in a profession that is an exclusive male preserve. And an ageing music teacher refuses to let poverty snuff out her dreams.

Underlying Nandita C. Puri's tongue-in-cheek humour and buoyant tone, is a rare perception of human nature. Her protagonists are women with minds of their own, driven by motives that are at times comprehensible, and at others, baffling — as full of surprises as life itself.

'*Nine on Nine* is fascinating because it is funny and full of life, the writing is a mixture of compassion and toughness, it is really political writing in the highest sense. The closest I can compare this book is to Edith Wharton's *House of Mirth*.'
— Mike Nichols, filmmaker, *Who's Afraid of Virginia Woolf, Graduate, Catch 22,*

'*Nine on Nine* is a beautiful collection of stories with exquisite insights into the human heart.'
— Gregory David Roberts, Author of *Shantaram*

'A well-told tale has the power to make the reader forget time and space and watch the line between fiction and reality blur as the characters acquire a life and momentum entirely their own. Almost all the stories in Puri's collection have the grip of stories well told and have a universal appeal that transcends gender or class. One can give *Nine on Nine* a perfect ten.'
— *Tribune* on Sunday

'The discerning powers of a journalist and the imaginative skills of a creative writer coalesce effortlessly to produce stories that are extremely readable. And disturbingly authentic. Puri's eye misses nothing.'
— Alpana Chowdhury, *Gateway*

'At the heart of each urban tale of questioning long established social questions, the stories are fairly interesting and make for quick reading.'
— *India Today*

'The book has a buoyant tone with tongue-in-cheek humour.'
— *Midday*

'Though thematically the stories explore different vistas of life, the milieu against which they are set and the attitude to life are quite similar because of their stark modernity.'
— *Jetwings*

'Nandita gets utmost satisfaction as a writer when she merges fiction with truth.'
— *Asian Age*

'The stories are simple and straightforward, studded with racy dialogues and written in a racy language.'
— *Today*

'The book has a rare perception of human nature.'
— Delhi *Mid Day*

'Despite their Indianness, these tales apply to many patriarchal societies in the world.'
— *New Strait Times*, Malaysia

Nine on Nine

Stories by
Nandita C. Puri

Rupa & Co

Copyright © Nandita C. Puri 2005

First in Rupa Paperback 2005
Twelfth Impression 2011

Published by
Rupa Publications India Pvt. Ltd.
7/16, Ansari Road, Daryaganj,
New Delhi 110 002

Sales Centres:

Allahabad Bengaluru Chennai
Hyderabad Jaipur Kathmandu
Kolkata Mumbai

All rights reserved.
No part of this publication may be reproduced, stored in a
retrieval system, or transmitted, in any form or by any means,
electronic, mechanical, photocopying, recording or otherwise,
without the prior permission of the publishers.

The author asserts the moral right to be identified
as the author of this work.

Cover: A sketch by M.F. Husain

Typeset in 12 pt Garamond by
Mindways Design
1410 Chiranjiv Tower
43 Nehru Place
New Delhi 110 019

Printed in India by
Gopsons Papers Ltd.
A-14 Sector 60
Noida 201 301

For the women who touched my life
...in general
And my mother
...in particular

Contents

Foreword	ix
Prologue	xi
An Arranged Marriage	1
At Jenny's	27
Flashback	55
Bhabhiji	72
Pages from Indulata Debi's Diary	98
Remembering Little Dee	117
Radha's Journey	141
The Piano Teacher	170
Waiting...	195
Acknowledgements	211

FOREWORD

Nandita Puri may look like a quiet, reserved person, but she is very eloquent with her pen. Absolutely talkative and unreserved. One hardly suspects that she observes so much, and so minutely, the realities which fly around her and quite often bruise her sensibilities.

She is honest and frank about her reactions and opinions in her newspaper columns. I have been an admirer always, but her short stories came as a revelation to me. I was not aware that she could fictionalise a reality with such expertise and hit the right chord. It will not be an exaggeration if I say that it is hard to draw the line in her short stories to separate fiction from reality and vice versa.

The character of Mrs D'Souza in *The Piano Teacher* is a result of superb craftsmanship. Or is it a direct reporting from life?

Pages From Indulata Debi's Diary is again remarkable for its form and style in telling the story. It is biography, history and yet a perfect form of a short story.

Another interesting aspect of her writing is the range of the cross section of society that she deals with and narrates so successfully. Her expression is precise and brisk. The details of the milieu in every story are remarkable for its region and class.

I think Indian fiction is richer by one more writer called Nandita Chaudhuri Puri.

Gulzar

Prologue

> *'Tis not enough your counsel still be true*
> *Blunt truths more mischief than nice falsehoods do:'*
> ALEXANDER POPE
> (An Essay in Criticism, III)

In the course of my career as a journalist and writer, I have encountered many strong (both actively and passively) women, which compelled me to put their stories down. And, in a way, also being a woman made sense to write about women, though of course gender has had no bias in my stories.

My stories are tales of men and women, of characters and situations. They span different cultural backgrounds, age groups and eras. Wittingly or unwittingly, consciously or subconsciously, I was to find out later that the underlying theme of my stories was the growth and spirit of women, mainly urban.

Perhaps one of the reasons could be that I have lived these experiences at one level or the other. Just like a travelogue, which has as much of the place as the traveller in it, so in my book, I travel through these various women's lives. Like a *sutradhar*. Therefore there is a bit of me in each one of them.

Nandita C. Puri

An Arranged Marriage

"Hello?" Rani picked up the phone on the third ring.

"*Aai?*"

"*Ho.* Rekha? *Kasa kay?*"

"*Bare.* What are you cooking?"

"Nothing much. Just a simple *khichdi*. I'll serve it with a plain *jeera raita*. Where is the time for cooking these days? After lunch your father and I have to go shopping. So many things to do. And so little time in hand. January 12th is almost here—less than a week away. We will be going to Kala Niketan. Want to join us?"

"Let me see. Rima will be back from school soon and after that I will have to sit with her homework," Rekha paused. "I thought you were through with your shopping. All you have been doing for the last few weeks is buying and buying. Now what is left to buy?"

"All this time we had been shopping for Anu and her family," Rani was referring to her future daughter-in-law, "Sarees for her mother and aunts and kurtas for her father and brothers. Then we had to get the bride's jewellery. Especially order the *mangalsutra* and the engagement ring. Now, we have to buy stuff for ourselves. We haven't even bought your brother's wedding suit. And he is the groom. Just imagine."

Rekha took a deep breath and sighed. "My! My! Aai. You guys are going crazy over Raja's wedding. But you never bothered at all when I got married. You never even came with me to buy my wedding saree. Remember? I had to take Bindya to help me select the saree. Then you and Baba made such a fuss over the price. It wasn't even expensive, but I felt so hurt that I wanted to return it. And now look at all the fuss you are making about your son's wedding? Especially over your future *bahu*. And to think I am your only daughter."

"Yes, yes. I know. But then who asked you to have a love marriage? You should have let Baba and me choose a boy for you. Had you opted for an arranged marriage, we would have made huge preparations for your wedding, like we are doing for Raja's," Rani told her daughter, trying to cover up her embarrassment.

"But Aai, Baba and you too fell in love and married against the wishes of your family, didn't you?"

"That is why our parents did not celebrate our wedding," Rani said.

"And so you decided to make me suffer the way you suffered by not celebrating mine?"

There was a pause. Rani had nothing to say to her daughter.

"It is not like that," she mumbled.

"Then what is it?" Rekha countered. "It is not that you two don't like Shiva. In fact, Baba gets along better with him than he does with Raja. He always did. And yet he did not actively participate in our wedding celebrations. Why the hypocrisy?"

"It is not hypocrisy...you don't understand..."

"Of course I do. You just found an excuse to cut costs on your daughter's wedding. True. Isn't it?"

"*Kya faltu baktue?*" Rani said, with growing exasperation. They had had this conversation several times earlier. But today Rekha seemed a little more upset than usual. She had always felt that she had had a raw deal. With Raja's wedding, the decade-old wound had started to fester again.

"*Faltu nako,* Aai. It is the plain truth. And it hurts."

"Yes. Yes. I know. But what could we do? It was all your fault."

"What do you mean, my fault?" Rekha asked.

"You chose Shiva, we did not. So why should we spend on your wedding?"

"But Aai, this is ridiculous. What if the boy you chose for me turned out to be a rascal? And how do you know that your future daughter-in-law may not turn out to be one?"

"*Ab bas karo*. You should learn to hold that tongue of yours. Do you want to come with us or not?" Rani told her daughter angrily.

"No. Both of you can enjoy your shopping spree for your *ladla*. I'll stay out of all this." With that, Rekha banged the phone down.

"*Deva re*. When will this girl grow up?" Rani said to herself as she put the receiver down on the cradle and flopped down on a chair. Rekha had always had a sharp tongue. As a child, she had constantly fought with Raja, who was five years younger than her. During her growing up years, it was with her parents, mostly her mother. And now she fought with her husband Shiva, and when he was not home, she vent her anger on her maids. Or her daughter Rima. Many a time, the poor child did not know why she was being yelled at or spanked. No wonder Rima preferred spending time more at her Nani's.

In a way, Rani had been glad when Rekha decided to get married. Though she did not show it, she was relieved when Rekha decided to marry a boy of her own choice. Thank God, they did not have to select a groom for her. Otherwise what would they have said to her in-laws when the latter complained about her. Bickering with her husband in public. Rani wondered what would have happened had she herself behaved the same way with Girish.

She had been a good wife for the past three decades. And obedient too. She seldom gave Girish reason for any outburst. And in his own way, Girish was also a good husband. Though demanding and quite austere in his tastes, he was a caring husband and a loving father. A disciplinarian no doubt, but a man of firm principles.

Rani remembered the time when she had first met him, almost thirty-five years ago, at the bus stop near her parents' house in Parla East. She and her cousin Shivani shared a rickshaw to college—the National Girls' College at Khar, where both girls studied Home Science. Girish would be waiting for his bus, Number 229, which started from Andheri and would take him to his office at Nariman Point, where he worked in a sharebroker's firm—Chagganbhai & Sons.

Though they did not exchange a single word for several months, the young man in his neatly pressed *kurta-pajamas* and well-worn Gandhi chappals soon caught Rani's eye. With his pleasant, smiling countenance, he was striking without being exceptionally handsome. He must be a few years older to me, she had thought to herself.

One day, the ice was broken. Rani was at the bus stop unaccompanied, as Shivani was not well. While she waited for a rickshaw, she had the feeling of being watched. Suddenly she saw the young man with the Gandhi chappals looking at her unabashedly. At nineteen, Rani, fresh-faced and light-eyed, made quite a pretty picture. Caught staring, Girish broke into a shy smile and Rani could not help but reciprocate. Girish casually walked up to her and enquired, "Your friend isn't with you today?"

"Oh, Shivanitai? She is my cousin. No, she is not well. Has a bad cold."

"So you are all alone? Where do you have to go?"

And thus it started. One question led to another and another. And this went on for the next few days, all those days when Shivani lay home in bed nursing a bad cold and fever. I hope Shivani stays at home for a few more days, Rani thought to herself. Anyway, she was so dismissive about Girish.

"So what is up with you and Girish?" Shivani asked her cousin.

"Nothing. We are just friends. That is all."

"Listen, don't try these games with me. Don't you notice the way he looks at you? He is in love."

"It is not my fault if he feels that way. I am only being friendly. Besides, I think it is all in your imagination."

"Tai, can I make a request?" Rani asked Shivani suddenly.

"What?"

"Will you promise not to tell anyone at home about Girish? Please."

"Oh. I see." Then with a naughty grin Shivani said, "Alright. But what do I get in return?"

"What do you want?" Rani asked apprehensively.

"Let me think. Hm... okay... maybe a weekly treat?"

"Uhh. Okay. As you wish." Rani was relieved.

Two years later, all hell broke loose in Sai Krupa, the Kulkarni family mansion.

"I will have none of this nonsense. Listen to me carefully, girl," Sandesh Kulkarni told his daughter Rani. "You cannot marry this Girish boy. What did you say his last name is?"

"Damle," Rani proffered meekly.

"Damle. See, he is not of the same caste as us. How can you marry him?"

"But Baba, he is Marathi...same province."

"Look Rani, I do not care whether he is a Maharashtrian or not. He does not belong to the same caste as us. He is not as rich as us. Can he give you a comfortable life—the life you have been used to in this house?"

"But Baba, he is still young. Only twenty-five. He has a lot of time left to make good. He is very hard-working and not doing too badly now."

"Alright. Alright. Enough of it. He may be a bright boy but I do not approve of your marrying him. No girl in our family has had the audacity to choose her own husband. We do not approve of such marriages...what do you call them, Shivani? *Lowe. Lowe* marriage. You will have to marry a boy we elders in the family select for you. Understand?"

"But kaka, what is wrong in Rani marrying Girish? He is a nice boy. I have met him..."

"Enough. *Bas kar*. I know all about it. Meeting at the bus stand and all. And you shielding her all along. You should have told us at the beginning. Then it would not have gone this far...see she wants to marry him now. You did not behave like a responsible sister at all."

"But what is wrong in Rani choosing her own husband? So many love marriages are taking place these days. Why, even Latatai married her..."

"You don't take that girl's name in this house. Utterly scandalous. And I will not have my daughter follow in her footsteps. Just imagine what will everyone say—*Kulkarni cha mulgi* has married out of caste. Had a bus stand romance. I will be the laughing stock of the neighbourhood. How can I show my face to people after this?"

And finally, to her family's utter horror, Rani eloped with Girish. They had a registered court marriage. A fortnight after that, Rani's father hosted a small reception for the bride and groom, comprising immediate family members and a few close relatives. Rani did not even call her friends. The reception was given more as a face-saver for the Kulkarni family. To stop tongues wagging about the "Kulkarni *mulgi's* elopement".

The Kulkarnis were well-off and their family mansion was the largest in the entire neighbourhood, comprising thirty large rooms spread over two storeys, with a large lawn at the back. Apart from the antique *sankheda* furniture, which Sandesh Kulkarni had specially ordered from Baroda, the house was famous for the two-hundred-year-old silver *jhula* which swung in the living room. It had engravings from the Ramayana on it and was said to have once belonged to the royal family of the Gaekwads.

All Rani got for her marriage was a plain gold necklace with matching earrings, two bangles and a red and purple *paithani* saree that had belonged to her grandmother and which she wore for her wedding reception. The feast was as frugal as the bride's ornaments, consisting of simple vegetarian Maharashtrian fare. Rani wondered what would happen to the rich collection of silk sarees and gold ornaments her mother had collected for her over the years and which was to be part of her trousseau. "They will go to your younger sisters. Who told you to marry out of caste? Why did you not settle for an arranged marriage? Stupid girl," Aai had admonished her.

This did not bother her as much as what her father made her and Girish do. Sign away her share of the family property. "So that you have no claim on my property," Sandesh Kulkarni explained to Girish when the latter looked surprised. "I hope you understand, son. I don't want people to say that you married my daughter for her money."

"But I do not want your money. I only want to marry your daughter," Girish had said self-righteously.

"I know. I know. But just to be sure."

"Don't worry, Rani," Girish had assured her later. "You need not feel bad. I understand your father's sentiments. But someday, I will earn enough so that you can live like a princess. Just like you did in your father's house."

And Girish Damle did keep his word. Though he did not achieve Sandesh Kulkarni's legendary wealthy status, he nevertheless tried his best. Today Rani had a four-bedroom sea facing apartment in the posh Juhu suburb. A bungalow in Lonavala with a small garden. And a farmhouse with two acres of land in Karjat. Several cupboards full of sarees from virtually every state of India. And a few bank lockers full of jewellery. "So that you don't feel shortchanged by your parents," Girish had told her off and on.

Rekha banged the phone down, visibly upset and muttering to herself, "Sometimes I hate her for the way she loves to hurt me. I don't understand why she does it? After all, she is my mother."

"*Ab kya ho gaya* between mother and daughter?" Shiva asked as he came out of the bathroom. "Back at it, you two?"

"Now you don't start off." Rekha was irritable.

"*Arre* Baba, I was just concerned about you. All well?"

"No. How can it be?"

"Why?"

"Look at the way Aai-Baba are throwing around money for Raja's wedding. And Baba wouldn't lend me money when I saw that flat in Lokhandwala. Said he was broke. Now where has all the money come from?"

"Maybe the old man has won a lottery? What they call it—Play Win or some such thing," Shiva said, while drying his hair with a towel. Seeing his wife glaring at him, he quickly gave her a hug. "Hey, I'm only joking."

Rekha could not help smiling at her handsome husband. Shiva, with his casual good looks and pony tail, had stolen her heart some fifteen years ago. She had been in school then. They had dated through her college years. He was like most young dudes, happily unemployed. Her girlfriends had envied her for hooking him. Quite a stud, they all agreed. And Rekha was ecstatic.

By the time she completed college, Shiva had landed an exciting job with the local music channel as a production controller. The pay packet was reasonably good.

"Lucky girl. Good catch. *Abhi fasao hero ko. Kisi tare bhi*," her friend Smita had advised her then.

"*Arre* no. Can't do. Besides Aai-Baba will not allow a love marriage. I will have to settle for an arranged marriage."

"Yeah. Sure. To some sissy *ghati* guy," Smita had taunted.

"*Nako, nako. Ata mi majhi mulgi barobar asa nai karnar.* We cannot do this to our daughter. I don't agree with you at all on this."

"*Isme agree ka baat kaha aye?* You do not have to agree. But you have to do it as a duty. On principle," Rani said to her husband.

Rekha overheard her parents arguing from her room.

It was only last evening, after dinner that Rekha had broken the news to her parents about her decision to marry her long-time sweetheart Shiva. Though the Damles were aware of their daughter "seeing Shiva", Rekha knew it would be difficult to convince them. Her father was already on the lookout for "eligible boys from the community" for her, whilst her mother was putting her trousseau together. Every time Rani liked a particular piece of ornament at a store, she would insist on Girish buying it for her daughter. "Don't you have enough already?" Girish would ask. "You hardly get to wear what you already have." "*Arre* Baba, *tumala kai vaatto, he majhe sathi?* You think it is for me? I am buying it for Rekha. Don't forget your daughter is of marriageable age. When we find a good match for her, how do you think we are going to produce her dowry overnight?"

When Rekha told her parents about her decision to get married, Girish Damle had been silent except for a faint "Oh". But Rani had exploded, "But how can you marry him? He does not belong to the same caste. He is a Mallu." Girish had indicated to his wife to remain silent. "*Aami nantar varta karua.* We will talk about it later." And now when the household had settled to afternoon quietness, Rekha in her room and Raja away in college, Rani broached the topic of her daughter's decision to her husband. The high decibels, Rekha gathered, must be because of that.

"What duty are you talking about? To deprive my daughter of her rightful share? She is your daughter too. How can you say such a thing?" Girish sounded greatly upset.

"But do you remember how I was deprived of my share for marrying you? Inspite of the fact that you were a Maharashtrian."

"But that was a long time ago, Rani. Those days were different. Besides, just because you have been deprived by your parents, you don't have to behave in the same way with Rekha."

"No. It is not fair. *He bara nahi aahe.*"

"*Kai bara nahi.* What is not fair?"

"Rekha marrying Shiva. In our community if girls don't settle for an arranged match then they are deprived of their share of the family property."

"Yes, I know. But I don't advocate it," Girish said.

"Why not? You will be depriving Raja of his rightful share."

"What do you mean? Raja will still have plenty after Rekha gets her share. In fact more."

"No. It's not just that," Rani argued. "He might question us about this later."

"That lazy rascal has no right to question us. It is my money, not his."

"You don't understand." Now it was Rani's turn to sound upset, "*Tumala kalat nahi.*"

"Wonder what the old man wants from you now," Rekha muttered to Shiva under her breath.

"Sshh," Shiva nudged her, "He'll hear you."

Even Shiva wondered why Mr Damle wanted to meet him suddenly that evening. After all tomorrow was the wedding. His and Rekha's. Inspite of all odds, they had decided to get married. Both sets of parents were dead against their decision. Shiva's mother too was very disturbed by the fact that her eligible boy was not having an arranged marriage with a girl of her choice. Worse still, she was going to miss out on a huge dowry. The stingy Damles were not going to give their daughter any dowry—they had already told the couple that they would have nothing to do with the wedding since it was not an arranged, but an inter-community marriage.

Inspite of opposition from his relatives and wife, Girish decided to host a small dinner party at the Sai-Krishna Hall in the local Krishna temple premises. Only fifty people would be invited, Rekha was informed. Girish and Rani's immediate family and a few close friends of Shiva's and Rekha's. "Now don't call your entire college *paltoon*. My funds are limited. I have organised limited dinner. We do not want any embarrassment." Girish had warned his daughter.

"What would you like to drink?" Girish asked his future son-in-law.

"Nothing, Uncle."

"Relax beta. You and me have a long way to go," Girish said as he poured two whiskies for Shiva and himself. Handing him a glass he said, "Here. Cheers. To the years ahead."

"Cheers," Shiva said as he sipped his drink awkwardly. This was the first time he was having a drink at the Damles'.

Wonder what the old man is upto, Rekha thought to herself. He is never so generous with his expensive Scotch.

After a few drinks, Girish brought out what looked like a stamp paper with some matter typed on it. "Here, beta. I want you to read this carefully," he said, passing it on to Shiva.

"What is it?"

"Just a formality. Disclaiming any rights to my property. Even Rekha will have to sign it. You see, daughters do not have any claims on their parental property if they do not opt for an arranged marriage. This is the system in our community," Girish explained, embarrassment visible on his face.

"Holy shit," Rekha almost blurted out. "I hope Shiva doesn't get upset over this," she thought to herself as she looked pleadingly at her future husband.

Hurt and humiliation was etched on Shiva's face. He reached for the pen and paper and asked coldly, "Where do I have to sign?"

Rekha heaved a sigh of relief.

"Thank you son. Now you have to sign here too," Girish said, gesturing to his daughter.

Rekha lost no time in picking up the pen and signing.

"I hope you did not mind, son. It is just a formality..."

"Why should we mind Baba. On the contrary, I am glad we signed. Shiva hates to be called a *ghar jamai*... Isn't it so, honey?"

"*Tumi chup raha*. I did not ask you."

"It is alright, Uncle. She echoes my sentiments."

"Raja, this will not do. *Yeh nahin chalnar*. She can have her parents visiting her once in a while but not her entire horde of relatives. Have I opened a *dharamsala* or what? Her people walk in whenever they feel like it. Uncles, aunts, cousins, cousins' cousins—just about anyone. Where have they sprung up from? We did not see half of them at the wedding," Girish Damle admonished his son.

"I know...." Raja muttered something incoherently, "I will tell her not to invite her relatives in future."

"You see, in our community the girl's parents visit her but do not stay in her in-laws' house. It is just not done. Such a shameful thing to do," Rani joined in as she came in from the kitchen.

"I know Aai," Raja muttered in embarrassment.

"I do not even encourage my brothers to stay with me when they come on their annual visit from the US. Because once you encourage this, an annual visit will become bi-annual and then quarterly," Girish said.

"*Hanh, kay nahin*. Everyone likes to be a houseguest. *Phukat mein khana-paani* plus they get free maid services here. That is why I don't encourage even Shivanitai when she comes here from London every two years. *Ek baar araam bhetla to...*" Rani nodded.

"I don't think Anu's parents will take advantage of us. It is just that since she is newly married and she misses them... and they miss her..." Raja tried feebly to stand up for his new bride.

"*Nakko re*. They are taking advantage of our hospitality. Now you don't have to support your in-laws blindly," Rani told her son.

"Aai why should I support them blindly. It is you and Baba who chose Anu. You knew her family. Then?"

"Listen, we did not foresee such hassles. Besides, your mother is not keeping too well. She already has high BP. She cannot take care of guests all the time. Please make it very clear to her parents and relatives, that they are welcome to visit their daughter, they can take her out, drop in here for a cup of tea. But if they want to stay in Bombay, they should make arrangements. Not in my house. Is that clear?" Girish was firm.

"*Hanh*, Baba."

"Tell them to stay at the *Hare Krishna Mandir*. They have nice clean rooms and are quite cheap. The food is also good there. Shivanitai always prefers to stay there on her visits," Rani added helpfully.

Thank God Anu decided to go out for a walk, Raja thought to himself. Imagine, poor girl, she would have been so embarrassed. But he realised his parents were right. They had been married for only two months now and the Damles had already played host to about thirty of Anu's relatives in this short period. Raja had never seen so many houseguests in his entire life. Apart from the pressure on his mother, Raja realised that he was also losing out on his privacy. This had to stop.

"Rima, stop pulling at my dupatta," Rekha snapped at her daughter.

"*Bas kar. Rahu dia. Bachchi hai.* At her age you were such a handful," Rani told her daughter as she rolled out a neat, round dough for the *karanji*.

"Yeah, I know," Rekha replied as she put the coconut and jaggery filling into the dough, and sealed the edges with delicate twists at equal intervals. Rani looked on in admiration. It was her mother who had taught Rekha to make *karanjis* and Rani till date felt that her daughter made even better *karanjis* than herself.

"*Achcha*, Aai. Remember when we had gone to Pune to see Anu for the first time? You and Baba had asked her whether she could cook? And remember what she had said?"

"What?" Rani asked.

"That she is very good at making *karanjis*. And her parents said that her *karanjis* were famous in the neighbourhood."

"*Hanh*, so?"

"This is your dear daughter-in-law's first Ganapati. She should be at her *sasural*, feeding you her legendary *karanjis* and *modaks*."

"*Achcha, bas kar.* You know she has gone to her parents," Rani said.

"She is forever visiting her parents. It has been hardly eight months since she got married and look at the number of times she has been to Pune. More than twenty. Looks like she spends more time there than here. Then why get married in the first place?" Rekha asked her mother. Rani knew her daughter was right. She could not think of a suitable answer.

"Aai, you and Baba should do something about it. First it was her parents visiting her and now she visits them so often. *Kya matlab?*"

"*Achcha rahu de.* You mind your own business," Rani told her.

"That I will. But all I was saying is that what is the point of having a daughter-in-law if she is not around to take care of you. All your life you have worked like a dog for your family—your husband, children. Cooking and keeping house. And now when you have a *bahu*, you are cooking and cleaning for her. What's the point?"

"*Tumi chup kar.* I know what to do," Rani told Rekha.

"Of course you don't. You cannot stand up to your son and *bahu*. You cannot say anything because you chose her. So now you put up with her. Next time you want a cook, call your chosen daughter-in-law, not your outcast daughter." Saying this, Rekha stormed out of the kitchen.

"Hi Shiva," Bindya waved cheerily. "Long time no see."

"Hi Bindya. Yes, I have been very busy. Work, work and work."

"I know. Rekha keeps me informed. But it's good to be busy."

"Yeah, I guess so."

"What's all this?" Bindya gestured at the furniture lying around in the building lobby and a large tempo parked nearby, "Someone's moving?"

"Yeah. My mother-in-law."

"Really? When? Where? This is news to me. How come I didn't know inspite of living in the same building?" Bindya asked, surprised.

"Yes...actually they wanted to be discreet about it," Shiva explained. "They are planning to settle down in Pune. Most of the furniture has been shifted already. This is the last lot. They are supposed to vacate the flat today."

"Oh dear!" Bindya sighed. "I will miss them so much. Ganapati won't be the same without Aunty's *modaks* and *karanjis*. I will miss her *puranpolis* too. And most of all I will miss Rekha. Atleast I would catch up with her in the lift or lobby when she came visiting. Now obviously she will have no reason to come."

"But you can always visit us. We are just around the corner. Besides, we will come over to your place if you invite us."

"Oh, c'mon now. As if Rekha and you need an invitation to visit me," Bindya smiled. "Oh, I must go and tell Mummy. She will be very upset when she hears this. As it is, Aunty had become such a recluse after Uncle's death. Mummy used to really miss her at card parties. She had always hoped that Aunty would get over her grief and start socialising soon. And now she is going away for good."

Shiva smiled.

"Say hi to Rekha and tell her to drop in sometime. How is Rima?"

"She is fine. Getting naughtier by the day," Shiva said, adding, "I will ask Rekha to call you up."

"Do that. Are you also going to Pune?"

"Yes. I will be dropping them. I'll return tonight. See you."

"Bye."

"Hello, Rekha? Bindya here."

"Hi there. Long time no see. Where have you been?"

"Travelling. Been to Singapore twice already in the last three months. Too much of travel is getting to me. I need a break."

"Good. Come and babysit my daughter for a few days. Too much of sitting at home is getting to me. I am bored to tears. I need to break free. Let's swap jobs. And you can have Shiva too as part of the package for a few days," Rekha said. Both girls laughed.

"Very funny. Stop joking," Bindya said.

"No. I am dead serious. I have had enough of marriage and motherhood. Ten years is way too long," Rekha said rather seriously.

"*Ab chor na yeh sab batein*. The reason why I called was I met Shiva in the morning and he said that your mother had sold the flat and was moving to Pune? Came as quite a surprise I must say. No one in the building knew of her plans. Strange."

"You are telling me. Even I was informed only a week ago. And that too because they needed Shiva to run around and help them with the shifting," Rekha said.

"But why all this secrecy? Anyway it is her decision and no one would have dissuaded her," Bindya asked.

"The problem is that it was not her decision to move. She has been forced into moving."

"I don't get you."

"You see," Rekha elaborated, "After Baba's death, Raja and Anu wanted to shift to Pune. This was basically Anu's idea as she wanted to be closer to her parents and relatives. I had warned Aai not to fall into the trap. But you know her—she thinks the world of her son and will do anything he says. Without telling Shiva and me they sold off the flat. Then Raja insisted Aai give him half the share of the sale proceeds, though Baba had nominated her in his will. But again, according to the Hindu law, the children are entitled to an equal share in case of sale of property. Since I had signed away my share at the time of my marriage, Raja and Aai shared the proceeds."

"I see," Bindya said while Rekha paused for breath.

"Well, that is not all. Aai is a Mumbai person and all her friends and relatives are here. She did not want to go to Pune but Anu made life so miserable for her that she was forced to say yes. This would not have happened if Baba was alive. But wait, the worst is yet to come."

"What do you mean?" Bindya asked.

"Listen to this then. Just yesterday she confessed to me that the Pune house has been bought entirely with her share of the sale proceeds while Raja has put his share in a fixed deposit jointly with Anu."

"Oh dear!" Bindya sighed.

"And here is the juiciest bit. Raja has made Aai register the house in his name. Can you imagine how stupid my mother is? Talk of blind love..."

"Dear me! Rekha, all this does not sound very good to me. Looks like Aunty is losing it..."

"Losing it?" Rekha cut in. "I think she has completely lost it."

"Aren't you worried about her?"

"Worried? I am totally pissed..."

"Is the sugar okay? Want some more?" Rekha asked Bindya as she passed her the plate of *khakras*.

"Absolutely perfect. Reminds me of old times. I do miss our *chai* and chat sessions," Bindya told Rekha. "But tell me Rekha, why does Aunty look so dazed these days? The other day when I met her in the market, she looked spaced out and barely recognised me. Even today, she didn't even acknowledge me. All's well with her, I hope?"

"It couldn't get worse," Rekha sighed.

"*Kya matlab?* I don't get you."

"You know how Raja and Anu made her sell the Bombay flat and buy the Pune house? Then they made her sign off that house in Raja's name. Aai could hardly settle down in Pune. New place, no friends, you know it is difficult to adjust at that age. But then she kept quiet about it.

"One day Raja started packing their stuff. When Aai asked him he said that they were going to the US for a holiday and that she should also pack her bags. She did. When they reached the airport, Raja took away all their boarding cards under some pretext. After a while, Anu too disappeared. Aai waited and waited till she realised that the flight had left.

"Thinking there was some misunderstanding, she returned home. Only to find that the house had been sold off without her knowledge and the new owners had just moved in."

"What are you saying!" Bindya gasped.

"Yes. It is true. She was completely devastated. She went to Anu's parents' place and they refused to entertain her. She called us and before I could fire her for her stupidity, Shiva snatched the phone from me and told her to take the next train to Mumbai. He picked her up from

Dadar and brought her straight home. Aai, he told her, my house may be small but I have enough place in my heart for you. Now this is your home. Rima of course was over the moon to have her Nani around. But Nani is not the same anymore."

"Obviously. I do understand. Such a terrible betrayal. I cannot imagine Raja doing such a thing," Bindya said.

"It is not the betrayal of her son which has affected her so much," Rekha said with hurt.

"Then what?" Bindya asked.

"The fact that she has to be dependent on her daughter for the rest of her life. Especially a daughter she does not like...."

"Come on now, Rekha. Don't be so harsh. After all, she is your mother. It is just her way of expressing..."

"I am not a child, Bindya. You know and I know, how much love she has for me. Her son's betrayal she can deal with...but being obliged to her daughter for the rest of her life, is something she has yet to come to terms with."

AT JENNY'S

"HI, JENNY. HI, MARGARET. ANYONE FREE? WANTED A shampoo and blow dry." Sonika, effervescent as ever, breezed in.

"Hi, Sonika," Jenny returned. "The girls are busy right now, but Shabana will be free in about ten minutes. Will you wait?"

"Yeah, I guess so," Sonika shrugged, as she sank into the sofa and picked up a copy of *Elle*, flipping through it casually.

Sonika had been visiting Jenny's Beauty Parlour for almost a decade. Ten years ago, when Sonika Gill's first job brought her from Delhi to Bombay, she was introduced to Jenny by her friend Damini. She could recall Damini's exact words to Jenny. "Jenny, this is my dear friend Sonika. I have recommended you highly to her, so please do not disappoint her." Then turning to Sonika, Damini had said, "You know, at Jenny's you get the best head massage in this city. So put away all your work worries and just chill."

And almost a decade later, Sonika Gill Shah still agreed that at Jenny's you got the best oil massage in town. As well as great pedicures and stylish haircuts. In short, the works. So without fail, once every week, Sonika would come to Jenny's for her weekly pedicure and head massage. And every once in a month she would have her (as she put it) "overhauling" done—full waxing of the arms, legs, underarms, upper lip and bikini line; eyebrow plucking; a pedicure and manicure; a herbal facial with skin rejuvenation; an oil massage, steam and shampoo followed by a hair trim and blow dry.

This monthly overhauling took a good four hours. But Sonika did not mind. In fact, she loved this monthly indulgence, when she could get away from home without having to give too many explanations for her absence. She enjoyed the girls fussing over her as they slapped various creams and lotions over her body, which moved along with the rhythm of their hands. Her husband, Viren, knew she would be in the parlour. She would switch off her cell phone and only Viren could get in touch with her at the parlour. That is, if it was really urgent. She had explicitly told him so.

Earlier, Viren would call up with the silliest excuse to check on his wife. Sonika revelled in his possessiveness, though it became quite irritating after a while. Soon the girls were instructed to tell Mr Shah that "Madame is busy, will call back" etc. Mr Shah's calls became less frequent till they stopped altogether. Thank God, Sonika had thought. For once I can relax without having to answer the phone or the doorbell. No *khitkhit* from the *bai* and no *bakbak* from hubby and kids.

"Going out for a party?" Jenny enquired, breaking into Sonika's thoughts.

"Well...not really. Going out for dinner at the Marriott. Today's our anniversary."

"Oh really! Congratulations." Jenny came over and hugged Sonika.

"Thanks," Sonika muttered.

"Congrats," Margaret chipped in while styling a customer's hair.

"Thanks, Margaret."

"How many years?" Jenny enquired.

"Eight," Sonika replied.

"Eight years! Well, it just seems like the other day that you came from Delhi. See how time flies. My, my."

"Yes. So it seems. Well, at least I have crossed the seven-year-itch," Sonika laughed her husky laugh. Everyone in the room joined in.

"So what did your husband give you?" Jenny asked.

"A watch. See," she stretched out her left wrist, showing off the brand new steel bracelet watch. "It is a Longines. La Dolce Vita," she added.

"Wow!" Jenny nodded, impressed. "I must say Mr Shah is quite thoughtful and generous."

"Well, I had to remind him at least ten times in advance about the anniversary. Shows how thoughtful he is. And as for generosity, well, we almost had a major showdown before he agreed to buy this. What more can one expect after so many years of marriage," Sonika grumbled.

"But he must love you very much," Jenny smiled at her. Sonika just smiled back.

"Don't worry honey, it is the same story everywhere. Men are like that," Petula looked up from her chair and at the mirror at Sonika's reflection. Margaret had just finished styling her hair.

"Oh hi, Pets," Sonika waved at her. "I didn't see you."

"Well, congratulations, my dear. If you ask me all husbands should be sent back to Mars. That is where they belong." Petula smiled.

"I totally agree," Sonika said. All the women had a laugh over that.

"I don't agree with you guys at all," Aalia, young and beautiful, suddenly piped up from her pedicure stool at the far end of the room.

"Really?" Petula asked, quite amused.

"Absolutely Aunty. Can you imagine life without men. No fun. Sooo bo...oring." Aalia said.

"Well, baby. You are too young to understand. Once you get married, you will see what I mean. Till then, have a good time and enjoy yourself as much as you can because this time will never come back."

"But Aunty, I can't wait to be married. My fiancé is such a sweetheart. He will make the most thoughtful husband," Aalia crooned.

"I am sure he will. Let us wait and see." Petula gave a knowing smile.

"Pets, why don't you leave the poor girl alone. Why dishearten her so early on," Sonika tried to intervene, laughing.

"But she should know the reality of it all," Petula argued.

"She will, in due course," Sonika said, smiling knowingly at Aalia. "Let her figure it out for herself."

"Oh! All you married women. You talk just like my mother," Aalia said.

"See baby, mama knows best," Petula said.

"Not true, Aunty," Aalia said as she finished her pedicure. "My dad is the most wonderful man in the world."

"Yes, all dads are wonderful so long as they remain dads and not husbands," Petula smiled.

"Aw..." Aalia gestured as she got up to leave. "We'll find out. Anyway, bye Aunty Petula, bye Aunty Jenny, bye Margaret, bye Shabana. See you, Sonika, bye." Aalia got up to leave.

"Bye," the others chorused.

"Hi, Aunty Jenny. Hi everyone," Aalia said as she breezed into the parlour a fortnight later. Then suddenly she looked at the mirror and caught sight of Sonika having a head massage. Shabana was gently rubbing her long lustrous hair with olive oil. "Hi Sonika!" she said.

"Hi, Aalia. How are you, my dear?"

"Fine. Enjoy your massage. I'll talk to you later," Aalia said, as she settled down for one too. She smiled at Radhika, who was busy warming the oil. "Gently, Radhika. Don't press hard, coz half my hair keeps falling," she warned in advance.

"Achcha baba, achcha," Radhika nodded as she started applying the oil on Aalia's hair. She then started pressing her head gently, as the oil seeped into her scalp.

"*Theek hai?*" Radhika enquired.

"Perfect. Bliss." Aalia crooned.

Half an hour later, as Aalia settled down for a pedicure, Sonika asked, "So, Aalia, how's life?"

"Great. Just back from Singapore."

"Work or holiday?" Sonika asked. She knew Aalia was working for the local MTV channel.

"Holiday. With my boyfriend."

"Hmm. Lucky girl," Sonika smiled.

"Well... you can say that again. We had a blast. I really enjoyed it. Lovely place and great for shopping. I'm sure you must have been there too?"

"Yes," Sonika said. "A couple of times, some years ago. Haven't been there lately though."

"How are Neha and Navin?" Aalia asked. Neha and Navin were Sonika's twins. "You don't bring them here anymore?"

"They are fine. You know how it is with children. They are much older, so I can now leave them with the *bai* at home. Besides, they are quite a handful," Sonika smiled. Aalia smiled too.

"And how is your jet-setting husband?"

"Oh, he is fine. Just returned from Singapore."

"You didn't go with him?"

"No. It was a business tour. He had to take some clients around. I get bored on such trips."

"Aalia, what does your fiancé do?" Petula asked one day. She was getting her hair dyed, while Aalia was getting her eyebrows shaped.

"Well, he has his own business. Also into stockbroking. I don't ask, Aunty," Aalia said.

"But you must check before you marry him. It is the most sensible thing to do. Don't you agree with me, Jenny?"

"Yes. Absolutely. That's what I keep telling her but she always seems to be in a dream world these days," Jenny replied as she streaked Petula's hair with another brushful of deep brown Majirel colouring.

"I can imagine," Petula laughed. "It is a heady feeling to be in love. No, Aalia?" Aalia smiled.

"How long have you been engaged, child?" Petula asked.

"Well...actually we are not officially engaged. Both the families are kind of against this match...so we are trying to keep it hush hush till things settle down."

"But why?" Petula persisted. Aalia was beginning to look distinctly uncomfortable.

"No...it's just that we don't belong to the same community. He is a Gujju and my folks insist I marry a Mangalorean. Besides, he is a lot older than me. Though that is hardly a reason. But try explaining that to my parents..."

"You mean to say your parents don't know about your boyfriend?" Petula asked.

"Not for the moment they don't. But I will tell them someday soon," Aalia replied.

"Well, you are old enough, my child. You know what is best for you. Just be a little cautious and don't let anyone take advantage of you, my dear," Petula said.

"Hi..." Sonika breezed in one afternoon. She caught sight of Mamta sitting on the sofa. "Oh hi, Mamta. Good to see you. Been quite a while."

"Hi Soni," Mamta said as she got up and hugged Sonika. "Good to see you too. It's been ages since we met last. I do miss our chats over coffee."

"Oh, yeah. Me too. I guess we've all got busy. Or just outgrown those coffee days," Sonika said.

"Well, at least I haven't outgrown it. But you definitely have become a busy bee."

"Well...the Citizen's Forum and the Mandala Destitute Women's Association...you know they sort of take up a lot of my time," Sonika said apologetically.

"I know," Mamta said. "I keep reading about you from time to time. You seem to have hit Page 3 big time."

"Oh that," Sonika gave a well-rehearsed, casual, dismissive wave of her hand. She turned to Jenny. "Jenny, sorry I am a little late. Is Shabana free?"

"Not to worry, dear," Jenny said. "Just give her a couple of minutes and she will be with you."

"No problem," Sonika said as she turned towards Mamta. "So. Are you in touch with the rest of the gang? How are Naina and Piroja?"

"Oh, not much these days. Piroja, you know, is in Beijing now. Kaizad has got a transfer there."

"Oh yes, I heard about it. God! Of all places China," Sonika said.

"But she seems to be quite liking it. In fact Lisa speaks good Mandarin. She is learning it in school," Mamta informed her.

"Oh. S...o...o cute," Sonika cooed.

"How are the twins?" Mamta asked.

"They are fine. And how is Ira? Which school does she go to?"

"Beacon High. Ira's doing good. Got the general proficiency award this year. Planning to go anywhere for the holidays?"

"Yeah. I am taking the children to London for three weeks. You?"

"Well, Moloy has some shoot in Baroda. So Ira and me will join him. Combining work with pleasure," Mamta said.

"But it is going to be bloody hot in Baroda," Sonika said.

"Well, yes. But then it is hot all over. Except of course in London. Isn't Viren going with you?"

"No. He is too caught up with work. Might just join us in the last week. But I would rather he did not. Half the holiday will be ruined. He and his Gujju food habits. Will spend half the time hunting for *dal-shak* and *tindoli-rotla* in London. And all I will be doing is lugging *khakras* and *chundo* or making *rotis* and *khatta-meetha* Gujju *dal* in the apartment," Sonika laughed. Both Jenny and Mamta joined in the laughter. "That way the kids are cool. Take them to McDonald's and they are happy and mama is happy. That is what I call a real holiday."

"Arre, did I tell you, Soni, I ran into Viren some weeks back. Did he tell you?" Mamta asked.

"No. Where?"

"At the Coffee Shop. The one in Juhu. He said he was grabbing a quick lunch."

"Grabbing a quick lunch in Juhu? His office is in Churchgate, why should he be grabbing a quick lunch in Juhu?"

"How would I know?" Mamta said. "He had a colleague with him. Introduced her as his secretary. Quite a sweet girl."

"Ah. You mean Mrs Mendonca. Sweet old lady," Sonika said.

"She was sweet but hardly old. No, I don't think her name was Mrs Mendonca. Atleast he said something like... Aishwarya...no, no. I can't remember. What was it?"

"Must be Rita. Rita Mendonca," Sonika added helpfully.

"No. No. I remember it started with an A," Mamta insisted.

"Never mind. You remember and tell me later. It must be one of those stenos then," Sonika tried to change the subject. She was beginning to feel a little uncomfortable. Jenny quickly came to her aid and asked, "When are you leaving for London?"

"Day after," Sonika smiled her best smile at Jenny, thanking her friend with unsaid words.

Radhika loved sitting by the parlour window and daydreaming. It had been six months since she joined Jenny's and this was her first job. Coming from a conservative Maharashtrian family, it was the first time in her life that she was away from home for so many hours together. While looking out of the window, Radhika noticed that she was being observed too. The person in question was a handsome young man she had noticed before. Always well-dressed, he wore a gold wristwatch and gold *kada* and behaved like a Hindi film hero. In fact, the girls jokingly referred to him as "hero".

Hero turned out to be Sonika Shah's driver and the girls later found out discreetly that his name was Raghu—Raghuvendra Singh.

"What caste is he?" Radhika had asked.

"*Bhaiyan hai, bhaiyan,*" Shabana had volunteered, meaning UP-ites.

"Arre, so sad. *Phir nahin jamega,*" Radhika seemed upset.

"*Kyon nahin*. Today inter-community marriages are so common. How does it matter? As long as he is interested in you, that is enough," Shabana had advised.

"*Arre* baba, you don't know my folks. They are very conservative. They will not even let me marry outside my caste, leave alone my community."

"Then that is your problem," Shabana had said.

Today Radhika was busy heating the wax on the stove by the window. From time to time she glanced outside. Suddenly she saw Raghu looking at her from the opposite side of the road where he usually parked the car.

"*Arre*, Shabana. Does Mrs. Shah have an appointment with you today?"

"No *yaar*. She is in London," Shabana replied, rubbing oil on her client's scalp.

"Then why is her car parked here?" Radhika asked, surprised.

"Where?" Shabana asked, craning her neck towards the window.

"There," Radhika pointed.

Shabana gave her a wink and said, "*Arre hanh*. You are right. Even her driver is there. Strange." She smiled.

"Maybe her husband is using the car. She told me he would be here," Jenny chipped in.

"But he has his own car. The BMW. Why would he take hers? He also has his own driver," Margaret added.

"Maybe his car is in the garage. And he must have given his driver a day off. Why bother?" Jenny said.

"Hello...everyone. This place is so..o..o cool. It is a furnace outside." Aalia walked in at that moment. And she was like a whiff of fresh air. The girls adored her. She laughed and joked with everyone and was always up to some prank or the other. Jenny just loved having her over.

"Come in, Aalia. How have you been? I always feel younger when I see you."

"Thank you, Aunty. And I feel so chilled out when I come here," Aalia added.

"I'm glad. Will you have a cold drink or a *chaas*?"

"No thank you, Aunty Jenny. I am in a bit of a rush. Have a lunch date you see," she winked at Jenny who smiled affectionately. "I'll just get my underarms waxed and run." Then turning towards Radhika, she said, "Radha baby, are you ready?"

"Yes. Yes," Radhika smiled as she picked up the bowl of hot wax with the steel tongs.

"Then let's go, baby," Aalia said as she headed towards the wax room.

"How is the new place looking? Have you settled in?" Jenny asked one of her regulars, Mrs Bhatia.

"Yes. Tomorrow is the *grihapravesh*...housewarming. We are having a *puja*. All my husband's relatives have come from Delhi. My brother and his family will be coming from Pune tomorrow. So much to do and so little time. I have kept an extra cook for three days to look after the food. My maid is getting her sister tomorrow to help. I am going mad!" Mrs Bhatia lamented.

"All the interiors done?" asked Mrs Parekh, another regular at Jenny's.

"Yes, more or less. Except the curtains and some bathroom accessories. I am getting a glass sink for Akash's room from Bhogilal. It is so expensive. Can you imagine, it costs thirty-five thousand rupees! A sink. And that too in glass," Mrs Bhatia said for the benefit of the entire parlour.

"I can imagine," Mrs Parekh joined her. "Money has no value these days. The other day, my son wanted to buy a pair of sneakers and can you imagine how much they cost? Twelve thousand rupees! For a pair of sneakers! And children nowadays don't value anything. Every six months he wants new shoes."

"How did Rahul's exams go?" Mrs Bhatia asked.

"Went off well. So he says. Let us see," Mrs Parekh said. "How about Akash?"

"Let's see. Nowadays he just sits at home and watches TV all day. And orders me to make this dish and that snack. I am so tired of cooking for both father and son," Mrs Bhatia said.

"Then just stop it and tell the *bai* to cook. Or better still, order from outside," Sonika looked up from her magazine. She was trying to read while getting her pedicure done, but she could not concentrate because of the two women's incessant chatter. This was nothing new. Every time Sonika found herself in the parlour with either Mrs Bhatia or Mrs Parekh, they spoke of nothing else but recipes and maids and children's exams and children's tuitions. Don't their lives have anything more than husbands and children, Sonika wondered to herself.

"*Arre*, what are you saying, Mrs Shah," Mrs Bhatia looked up at Sonika. "I cannot do that. My husband likes my cooking."

"So teach your *bai* your priceless recipes and mark my words, Mr Bhatia will not be able to tell the difference," Sonika said.

"How can that be? That will be cheating. Besides, my husband can tell the difference between my cooking and the maid's."

"Well, then it is too bad," Sonika said.

"*Arre* Kunika, I saw your photograph in the *Bombay Times* the other day," Mrs Parekh suddenly butted in. "You were in some rally, no?"

"No. And the name is Sonika, not Kunika," Sonika was suddenly icy.

"*Hanh*. Right. Sonika. I am sorry," Mrs Parekh said.

"That is alright," Sonika muttered.

"Tell me, Mrs Shah, aren't you married to the actor Sunny Shah?" Mrs Bhatia asked.

"No," Sonika was getting irritable.

"Oh. I am sorry. Then what does your husband do?" Mrs Bhatia asked.

None of your business you fat cow, Sonika wanted to say. But instead she smiled. "He is a stockbroker. Has his own firm," she replied, in her politest tone.

Walking into the parlour one evening, Sonika bumped into Aalia.

"Going?" she asked Aalia.

"Oh hi Sonika. Yes. Just finished."

"Why the rush?" Sonika asked.

"Actually I have a lot to do. Packing and all. Am leaving for London," Aalia smiled.

"Oh. I see. Going on a holiday?" Sonika asked.

"Well...sort of..." Aalia smiled.

"Well, enjoy your trip...have a nice time," Sonika said.

"Thanks. Bye everybody."

"Shabana, I want a blow dry. Quick. *Jaldi*."

"Yes, Mrs Shah. Just a minute," Shabana said, adjusting the chair, "Come. Sit here."

"Going for a party?" Jenny enquired.

"Not really. Just going pub hopping with some girlfriends. We want to chill out without the men," Sonika said.

"My, my. A girl's night out. Lucky you," Margaret said. "And what about hubby dear? Leaving him to babysit?"

"Oh, hubby dear is in London. On a business trip. That is why we girls decided to let our hair down. In fact two of my friends' husbands are also out of town," Sonika said.

It was one of those relaxed days at Jenny's. Sonika was taking a steam and getting her pedicure done, flicking through a magazine at the same time. Petula and Aalia were getting their heads massaged.

"Are Judy's results out?" Aalia asked Petula, who was half-asleep. Petula opened her eyes a couple of seconds later and looked at Aalia in the mirror.

"Sorry. What did you say, my dear? I almost dozed off. Shabana has this effect on me whenever she touches my head," Petula smiled as she looked up towards Shabana who smiled back. "Judy's results? No. They are not yet out. Should be out in a week's time."

"Pets, I quite agree with you on the Shabana bit. Every time her fingers touch my scalp, I am off to la la land," Sonika joined in, "Na, Shabana?"

"You guys must try Radhika too someday," Aalia interjected. "She is good too."

"Of course I have tried her," Sonika said, "she is excellent."

"Thank you Madam," Radhika smiled at Sonika who smiled back.

"Ouch. Praise you and it goes to your head. Softer, softer." Aalia suddenly exclaimed, putting up a dainty, manicured hand to gesture to Radhika to take it easy. Her fingers look so lovely and slim, Petula thought to herself. Look at mine, they look so bloated. Water retention. Shit. Wish I had slim fingers like this girl. How beautiful the diamond looks on it. Petula gazed admiringly at the diamond flashing on the third finger of Aalia's right hand.

"Hey. That is a nice ring, my dear. Very pretty. Show me?" Petula pointed towards the ring.

Aalia blushed a deep red as she stretched out her hand.

"Beautiful. Take it off and show me, will you?" Petula insisted. Then looking at Aalia blushing, she asked, "Gift from boyfriend? Lucky girl."

Aalia took off the ring and handed it to Petula.

"Wow! Pretty design. Is it platinum?"

"No Aunty. It is white gold," Aalia answered.

"Lovely. Look at the rock at the centre. Quite a size. Your boyfriend must love you very much to give you this," Petula commented while Aalia could not stop blushing.

"Let's have a look," Sonika said from her pedicure stool.

"Here, Margaret, can you pass this on to Sonika. Shabana's hands are oily."

Margaret could not help exclaiming, "Wow! Gorgeous piece. Must have cost a fortune? You have got yourself a rich boyfriend, girl."

"It is very pretty," Sonika said as she took the ring. It was a double band in white gold, studded with nearly fifty pieces of small, brilliant cut diamonds. The band held what looked like a massive solitaire, over a carat in size. But on closer look, one realized that it was a very clever bit of designing. Four princess cut diamonds, each weighing twenty-five cents were set together closely, in invisible setting, to give the effect of a solitaire. Brilliant.

"Here Margaret, give it back to Aalia please," Sonika handed her the ring. "Is it from Ishna?"

"Where?" Aalia looked blank.

"Oh, the jewellery boutique in Bandra?"

"I wouldn't know," Aalia said.

"I had seen a similar ring there," Sonika said.

"Could be. I wouldn't know. It is a gift," Aalia said.

Sonika recollected how, some months back, she had visited the trendy new jewellery store, Ishna. She had seen a similar ring and liked it instantly. What a clever bit of designing, she had thought to herself. Everyone will think

I am wearing a rock without having to pay the price of one. It was for around forty-five thousand rupees or so, if she remembered correctly. I'll tell Viren to buy it for me as an anniversary gift, she had thought then. She had shown him the design in the store's catalogue. Viren, of course, had refused outright. Too expensive, he had complained. I cannot afford it right now, as my business is not doing too well. Cheapskate, Sonika had called him, and sulked for days. Finally, to appease his wife, he had bought her a Longines Dolce Vita at half the price of the ring. Well, well, that is life, Sonika sighed.

"Oooh. I am so excited," Aalia cooed as she looked into the mirror at her hair. She had just done a highlight and was quite pleased with the results. But nevertheless, she wanted to be doubly sure. Just then she saw Sonika coming out of the facial room.

"Tell me honestly, how does this look on me?" she asked, gesturing towards her hair.

"Gorgeous," Sonika replied. "The colour suits you well."

"Serious?"

"Absolutely."

"Thanks, Margaret," Aalia turned to Margaret.

"You are most welcome," Margaret replied.

"Where are you off to now?" Sonika asked.

"Guess?" Aalia asked.
"I give up."
"South Africa."
"Oh, I see."
"We are going for the World Cup Finals. The India-Australia showdown."
"Great. Are you going with your boyfriend?" Sonika asked.
"Yes," Aalia blushed. "Actually he is taking me with him. One of his business colleagues in South Africa is sponsoring our trip."
"Lucky girl," Sonika said, "Even my husband is going to South Africa to watch the finals. Some of his friends have organised the trip."
"So why don't you go with him?" Aalia asked. "Then we can catch up and go out shopping together."
"No. It is an all boys' trip. Women not allowed. Also, the kids have school. Can't keep bunking every time. Besides, it's not much fun shopping in South Africa. Just local handicrafts and all that crap, you know?"
Aalia nodded. "So you have already been there?"
"Yeah. Once. About two years ago. We took the children on a safari. We did South Africa, Kenya, Nigeria and Swaziland together on that trip."
"Wow! That must have been really exciting," Aalia said.
"Yes, it was," Sonika replied.

"Looks like your husband and Aalia keep going to the same places. Last time it was Singapore, then London. One of these days they are going to bump into each other," Margaret said.

"Well...actually you are right Margaret, come to think of it," Aalia said.

"That's right. I hadn't thought of it either," Sonika said. "Hey, wait a minute. Let me give you my husband's cell number. You can get in touch with him and say you are a friend of mine."

"Just a second," Aalia said as she took out her cellphone. "Let me feed it in. Shoot."

"9819133001. It is a roaming number but you can only SMS. No calls. When he travels abroad, he prefers to take this...you know the number of local calls he has to avoid. SMS him and he will reply or call you back. Just a second..." Sonika reached for her cell phone from her purse. "I'll have to take this call outside. There is no network in here." She hurried out of the parlour.

Aalia looked after Sonika and shrugged. Crazy woman, she forgot to mention her husband's name. Anyway, how does it matter, she thought to herself. I am hardly likely to call him. I will be too busy to bother about calling anyone else. Nevertheless, let me just put the number down as Sonika's hubby. Hey wait a minute. 9819133001. Haven't I seen this number before? Looks kind of familiar. Ah, it was like Rohit's—9819100330. No wonder it seemed familiar. Both are pretty close.

"Hello, Mrs Shah. Good morning," Shabana wished Sonika as she pulled out a chair.

"Good morning Shabana," Sonika said, cheerfully, "Hi Jenny. Hi Margaret. Hi everyone. Nice day. Not too hot."

"Yes, it is always nice to have you as our first customer. It brightens our day," Jenny told her.

"Oh thanks, Jenny," Sonika smiled. "You really make me feel so good with all that flattery."

"No. I am not flattering you. It is the truth. Aalia and you really brighten up this place. I am not saying my other clients are not nice, but it is better to have a bubbly presence than have somebody cribbing about absent *bais* and fussy husbands," Jenny said. Sonika and the others knew whom she was referring to.

"Yes. That reminds me, where is that girl Aalia? I haven't seen her in a while. She didn't even get in touch with Viren in South Africa. I had asked him and he said no. How is she?"

"No news from her. In fact, she has not been here since she went to South Africa. Remember, you two exchanged some numbers?"

"Yes. Yes. But that is strange. She is quite regular, isn't she?"

"Without fail, she is here twice a week," Margaret said.

"It's been almost three months since Viren went to South Africa. By now Aalia's eyebrows must have become bushes," Sonika said.

"Unless she has found another parlour," Jenny said suddenly.

"But why would she do that? She was happy here, wasn't she? Unless, of course something went wrong," Sonika said.

"Well, nothing could have gone wrong from our side," Margaret wondered aloud, "But even if something did, then she should have told us so. I am sure she would have called."

"Let's call and check on her," Jenny said. "Just remind me Maggie."

"Alright."

"I have a feeling something is amiss. I have been so busy with Sunny's exams. Then my in-laws came to stay. It has been a very busy month," Jenny said.

"Hi. Good morning girls." It was Petula at the door.

"Oh hi, Pets. Good to see you. How have you been?"

"Super, darling. And you?"

"Fine," Sonika said. "We were just talking about Aalia. She hasn't come to the parlour in a while. Have you seen her recently?"

"No. This is the only place I meet her. I rarely bump into her otherwise. Once I saw her at the coffee shop at the Marriott with an older man. But that was many months back. I haven't seen her of late. Why don't you give her a call, Jenny, and find out?"

"That's what we were planning to do. I've left my diary at home. I'll get it during lunch time. What can I get you both? Some coffee, tea or *chaas*?"

"Thanks, but nothing for me," Petula smiled.

"What about you, Sonika?"

"I don't mind a cup of coffee."

"Sure. Priya, make a nice cup of coffee for Madam, with less sugar please," Jenny instructed one of her girls.

"So, my dear. How are the twins?" Petula asked Sonika.

"They are fine. And Judy? What is she up to these days?"

"Oh she's good. Is debating on whether to take up law or journalism."

"I'd suggest both," Sonika said.

"Very helpful, aren't you?" Petula smiled. "Hey, that's a pretty ring," she said, pointing to the ring on the third finger on Sonika's right hand, "But...wait a minute. Isn't it the same one Aalia was wearing?"

"Yes. Exactly the same one. Except, this one's mine," Sonia said, flashing it proudly.

"I never for a moment doubted that," Petula smiled at the younger woman, "I remember you mentioning that you had seen it somewhere."

"Yes, if you recollect I was telling Aalia that I had seen it in Ishna. You know, the new jewellery store in Bandra?"

Petula nodded.

"Well actually, Pets, I liked it the day I set my eyes on it. I had told hubby dear to buy it as an anniversary gift. You know husbands. He refused outright. Said it was too expensive and all that. Then after seeing it on Aalia, I happened to tell Viren that husbands tend to take their wives for granted. What he refused me, a young girl's boyfriend had got her...He pretended not to hear. But soon after the South Africa trip, a few days later in fact, he surprised me with this," Sonika flashed her finger once again.

"Wow! Lucky girl," Jenny said.

"Yes. I must say that was pretty thoughtful of him," Petula added.

"Yes," Sonika smiled softly. "It was quite touching. I would not have imagined he would actually remember the design. He had barely glanced at the catalogue when I first showed it to him."

"Oh, don't let these men fool you. With them, you never know," Petula said.

"I know, they are full of surprises," Sonika smiled.

A week later, Petula walked into Jenny's to varnish her nails. "Show me some nice colours, Priya," she said.

Shabana and Radhika were sitting by the window while Margaret sat on a barber chair, pretending to read the newspaper. It had been a dull day at Jenny's, with hardly a couple of customers.

"It's a *dhila* day today, isn't it, Jenny?" Petula looked towards Jenny sitting at the counter, writing something on a piece of paper.

"Yes. Exceptionally. Otherwise can you imagine Shabana and me sitting idle like this. It's always choc-a-bloc with appointments," Jenny said.

"Good to relax once in a while," Petula said.

"Well...yes...I guess so. But business is also important. I have overheads you know."

Petula smiled. She picked up a bottle of varnish from the tray and gestured to Priya to apply it on her nails. A thought struck her.

"Jenny, did you manage to speak to Aalia that day?" she asked Jenny.

"Well...yes...I did..." Jenny seemed a bit hesitant.

"What is it? Something wrong?" Petula asked.

"Well...how do I put it...I didn't like what I heard."

"What was it? What did she say?"

"Nothing. In fact I did not speak to her at all," Jenny said.

"Then?" Petula asked.

"Well...it is like this. Aalia was not home. Her mother picked up the phone. She was polite but sounded upset. When I mentioned that we were anxious about Aalia, she broke down. Apparently the family had no idea that Aalia was seeing someone. Nor did they imagine that she accompanied him on holidays abroad. She would tell them she was travelling on office work.

"Till she returned from South Africa. She broke down and confessed. Apparently she found out during the trip that he was married and had a wife and children and obviously had no intention of marrying her. He was just having a good time. She was heart-broken. She decided to take a break from the city as it had too many painful memories for her. So she has gone off to her native place—Mangalore. The Shettys are devastated by their daughter's behaviour. Aalia's mother was worried that it would be difficult to find a good Tulu boy for her now," Jenny concluded.

"Oh, poor girl. She must be feeling embarrassed to come here too. Considering how we used to rib her about her boyfriend. It must be so upsetting. Imagine playing with innocent hearts. Men are such bastards at times," Petula said, agitated.

"Mrs Shetty said he used to shower her with expensive gifts. He had apparently proposed to her and even given her an expensive diamond ring," Jenny said.

"Good, at least she got something out of this relationship—even if it is only a diamond. They last longer than men," Petula said.

"No. According to her mother, she threw the ring back on his face," Jenny said.

"What! Stupid girl!" Petula exclaimed.

Flashback

Srimoti was extremely beautiful. And arrogant too. And that is precisely what Champa hated about her.

Champa gawked at her secretly though. The way she flicked her fingers lightly and stylishly through her light brown silky tresses. Which, however hard Champa might try, she could not get her matted mane to emulate. Or when Srimoti walked around, flaunting her shapely legs, with her socks rolled down to her ankles and her hemline several inches higher than what the school rules prescribed. Champa stole glances at her firm, rounded breasts held by delicate straps, the contours of which were clearly visible through her cotton shirt on a hot day. At fourteen, Champa's breasts were still not big enough to fit the smallest cups available in the market, size 28A. She was beginning to get tired of those shapeless cotton slips. At fourteen, Srimoti wore size 32B.

At the assembly, Srimoti stood out in the crowd of students—tall and curvaceous, with perfect features, a glowing complexion, and skin that appeared to have been bathed in turmeric and milk. Her seniors envied her, her juniors idolised her. Or rather, her looks. For Srimoti was not the most amicable person on earth to be with. Beauty breeds arrogance, and Srimoti had her fair share of it. The only girl she was close to was Aparna. Aparna, of average intelligence, short, dark and fat, with a nose that resembled flattened cow dung. The only thing they seemed to have in common was Amitabh Bachchan. Both were diehard fans, always catching the first day, first show of all his films. They spent hours discussing his dance numbers in *Don* and his haircut in *Laawaris*. And god help anyone who passed the slightest uncomplimentary remark on their hero. With her acidic tongue Srimoti would reduce the person to tears.

Champa was at a loss to understand what had attracted Srimoti to Aparna in the first place. Especially when there were any number of girls who would have given their right arms to be seen with Srimoti. After all, the boys constantly ogled at Srimoti and anyone hanging out with her would merit at least a certain amount of attention. Whatever it was, Srimoti and Aparna's friendship was the butt of many a joke in Good Shepherd Girls' High School.

One day Champa came to school a little earlier than usual to find that none of her friends were around. She checked the time only to realise that she was a good twenty minutes early. Leaving her bag on her desk, she made her way towards the steps of the school building, from where she got a vantage view of the main gate, and sat down. That way, she could spot her friends the moment they walked in. Also, it was fun to watch the students arrive, in their vehicles or with escorts—parents, maids, or older siblings—or sometimes just by themselves. While the younger children usually clung to their parents' hands till they entered the gate and waved vigorously till they faded into tiny dots, the older girls tried to brush off their escorts in an embarrassed manner even before they reached the gate. After all, they were old enough to walk to school on their own, weren't they? Didn't kids in the US at fifteen and sixteen live on their own, away from their parents? "Why the hell can't my parents leave me alone" was writ large on their faces.

Casually Champa fiddled with her watch strap as she waited. It was a gent's watch, with big bold numbers, far too big for her skinny wrist. Hers was an old castaway, a gift from her favorite uncle.

Her parents would not buy her one as they thought she was too young to possess a wristwatch. She had to earn it, they told her. When children these days sported watches the moment they stepped in to kindergarten! Almost all her classmates wore a watch and the few exceptions did not like wearing one. Not because they did not own one. For days Champa's joys knew no bounds and she proudly displayed her new acquisition, an old Anglo-Swiss, several sizes too large. Six months later, when the romance of owning a watch had died down, it dawned on her how big and ugly it was and that it did not suit her wrist at all.

How she would have loved to have a dainty dial with a delicate gold strap, just like the one Srimoti flaunted. "It's a Citizen. My aunt got it from the US," Srimoti had casually let drop when Champa had commented on its cuteness. Why don't I have some relative in the States who'd pamper me with such gifts? Champa thought, when she heard a slight commotion at the gates. She looked up and saw it was Srimoti, getting down from her ancient-looking but nevertheless impressive Ford, causing a minor traffic jam, a daily affair.

Instead of heading towards her classroom, Srimoti walked towards the principal's office. Following close behind her was a short, dark, balding and slightly bent gentleman, somewhere in his mid-sixties. A dark suit hung limply on him. He was desperately trying to keep pace with Srimoti while she deliberately walked ahead, feigning not to know him. But of course, Champa had seen them get out of the Ford together, so obviously he was an acquaintance. As they crossed her, Srimoti suddenly gave her a friendly smile and an unexpected "Hi". It was such a departure from her normal routine that Champa could only gape and barely manage to nod.

She got up and headed towards the office too. Srimoti had already gone in with the gentleman A few minutes later they came out. Champa quickly planted herself in front of them with a big smile and curiosity writ large on her face. She could hear Srimoti telling the gentleman rather rudely, "Alright. Everything will be fine. Now go home quickly." Before she could finish, Champa butted in, "Your granddad?" she asked.

"No. My father," Srimoti admitted sheepishly. "*Bapi*, meet Champa. She's in my class."

"Hello uncle," Champa chirped.

"Hello Champa," returned Srimoti's father, diffidently, with a shy smile.

"You can go now. The car is causing a traffic jam outside. *Jao.*" And with that she turned and left, whisking Champa away before her father could say anything. It seemed like she did not want to be seen with him. And rightly so, thought Champa. The contrast was so evident. Beauty and the beast.

At assembly that day, Champa watched Srimoti with a certain smugness. She knew Srimoti was embarrassed about her father and did not want to be seen with him in the presence of her friends. Yet Champa had not only met him, but had also been introduced to him. And she also knew that Srimoti was not happy about this. She was suddenly being over friendly with Champa, to drive home the unsaid message—let's forget you ever met my father, pal, and don't talk about it to anyone. She suddenly felt one up on Srimoti.

Champa had seen and met Srimoti's mother several times. She did not resemble Srimoti even remotely. In fact, her dusky prettiness contrasted with her daughter's regal good looks. However, girls mostly take after their fathers and Champa had expected Srimoti's father to be tall, fair and good-looking. What she saw this morning was another story. Then where on earth did her complexion and good looks come from?

In a strange way that incident cemented a bond between Champa and Srimoti. Slowly they built up a friendship. The initial casual "hellos" extended to awkward chats, then longer chats and then even longer ones, till soon they were seen moving around together, along with Aparna. Initially Aparna resented the intrusion, but she reconciled herself to it for fear of losing Srimoti's friendship.

Champa realised that Srimoti was not such a bad person after all. She was a private person who liked to keep to a few good friends, which many mistook for arrogance. Her comments on people were wicked, but without any spite. What never failed to surprise her was Srimoti's bawdy sense of humour, totally at odds with her surface primness.

Like all teenagers, each of them had her fair share of crushes, though in Srimoti's case it was most often the other way round. One day, however, while having their usual tête-à-tête before the assembly, Srimoti blurted out that there was this extremely handsome guy opposite her house, who stared at her every time she came out on her verandah. "He's so good-looking that it's difficult to ignore him. I hope he hasn't caught me ogling at him. Not that I mind much."

"Where the hell did he materialise from? You never mentioned any good-looking neighbour all these years?" Aparna demanded.

"I myself didn't know that he existed. It has only been a few days since I first saw him standing on the opposite verandah. You know the Ghoses across? The ones who never speak to us, for some strange reason?" Srimoti asked Aparna. The latter nodded.

"At first I thought he was a family friend on a visit. But I saw him the next day and the next..."

"Did you bother to find out?" Champa cut in.

"Yes," Srimoti replied. "My maid filled me in with the details when I asked her. You know Lakshmi? What a gossip she is? Seems to know everything about every household in the neighbourhood."

"Tell us," said Aparna, eagerly.

"Well, his name's Arijit and he is the Ghose's only son. He's settled in the US. Works there. He's been there ever since his college days. He's done his MBA from an American university. Very brilliant, I guess."

"Then how come you've never seen him earlier?" Aparna asked.

"Because he hasn't been here for fifteen years."

"Fifteen years!" Champa exclaimed. "That's a hell-of-a long time. He must be quite old?"

"Thirty-fiveish. If you call that old." After a pause Srimoti drawled, "I think it's a very sexy age for men."

"Wow! Very Mills 'n Boonish," piped up Aparna.

"This is his first visit home since he left for his studies. It's his parents who have always visited him there," continued Srimoti. "Maybe he didn't come here earlier because of Green Card hassles and all. But Lakshmi says he was packed off to the States by old Mr Ghose because of some scandal."

"What scandal?" Champa asked.

"She said she didn't know the details. It was a long time ago. She couldn't remember."

"You better check out his past before you get into anything serious. You never know with these guys settled abroad. They always seem to have some skeletons tucked away in their cupboards," cautioned Champa.

"Well, first let me get to know him and then we'll check out his past. What are a few skeletons anyway? It definitely makes the guy more attractive *yaar*."

"But..." before Champa could say anything more, the bell went off for assembly.

Events, however, took a turn as Arijit called up Srimoti soon after and declared his interest in her. Srimoti tried to act nonchalant, but the older and more experienced man was quick to sense her interest in him. He expressed a wish to meet her but warned her to keep it to herself for the time being. "You know how parents can be about these things," he cautioned her in his American drawl. Since Srimoti's parents were very conservative, she decided not to tell them anything about the affair.

The girls were very excited for her and were keen to see how things progressed, but soon the school closed down for the Puja holidays. Aparna did not have a telephone at home and Champa's had been out of order for months. They couldn't be in touch with each other or monitor the progress of their friend's romance.

Aparna had gone to Srimoti's house once during the holidays and tried to enquire about Arijit. But the latter had glared at her, motioning her not to mention him in front of her mother. Since she was chirpy and had a distinct glow, Aparna assumed that all was going well on the romance front.

"*Subho Bijoya* and Happy Diwali, belated though," Champa waved and yelled out the moment she spotted Srimoti and Aparna.

"Thank you. Same to you," both returned in unison.

She noticed a glow on Srimoti's face and enquired, "Have I missed out on something?"

"I was just telling Apu about Arijit," said Srimoti.

"Tell me quick. What's been happening?" asked Champa.

"Oh everything's fine. We met, secretly though. I've gone out on several dates with him. He's very charming. Really witty," Srimoti raved. "He's great to be with. And boy, is he good looking! A real lady-killer. What a physique! He's almost six feet tall. And has such handsome and rugged features. Whenever we go to a restaurant, the women just stare at him."

There was a pause as Srimoti fiddled with a small heart-shaped pendant on a delicate gold chain round her slim neck. Both Aparna and Champa noticed it and the latter exclaimed, "Hey, that's beautiful."

"It's Arijit's present to me," Srimoti said shyly.

"Really? Gold?" asked Champa.

"Yes. 18 karat."

"Wow. This is getting serious. There must be more to this. Tell us, what did he do?" asked Aparna.

"What do you mean?" said Srimoti, feigning offence.

"Oh. Come off it. Tell us. We're dying to know," pleaded Aparna, "or do you want our imaginations to go wild?"

"Well he did hold my hands," smiled Srimoti.

"*Bas?* And?"

"And he caressed them."

"And?"

"And we kissed," Srimoti blushed furiously.
"How was it?" insisted Aparna
"Pleee...ase. Stop it," she pleaded.
"Alright. That's it," Champa said, coming to Srimoti's rescue. "We'll imagine the rest though," she winked at Aparna.

For Srimoti, it was her first serious involvement. She was completely besotted with Arijit. Arijit, on his part, treated her with affection. He tried to initiate a physical relationship with her, but stopped himself in time, perhaps because he realised how young she was. Soon it was time for him to leave, but not before Srimoti made him promise to write to her once a week and call her at least once in a month. "And if anyone else picks up the phone, just hang up," she warned him.

His letters were an extension of himself: charming and flirtatious. Srimoti would smuggle them to school tucked in her bra and proudly show Aparna and Champa the envelope with the slightly sweat-smudged scrawl, bearing on them the letters "Miss Srimoti Roy, c/o Sandhya Das". Sandhya maasi was Srimoti's aunt, much older to her but nevertheless sympathetic about her friendship with Arijit.

Srimoti read out the letters to her friends, omitting the more personal bits, and the girls noticed that she seemed in high spirits when his letters arrived. They were happy for her, though sometimes Champa would feel a pang of jealousy and secretly longed for someone to send her love letters too.

Gradually the letters became less and less frequent, and Srimoti got more and more edgy. Till one day she got so impatient that she decided to pay a visit to the Ghoses, something she had never done.

Mrs Ghose opened the door and was dumbstruck to see Srimoti. "Can I come in?" said Srimoti with her most charming smile.

"Please come in," Mrs Ghose was polite but curt. "Anything I can do for you?"

"No. I just came to say hello. I've seen you all these years and yet we've never spoken. So I thought I'd introduce my..."

"There's no need," cut in Mrs Ghose. "I know who you are. Anything else?"

"No. I mean...I was... no..."

As she turned to leave, a framed photograph of Arijit on the side table caught her eye. Feigning innocence she turned to Mrs Ghose and said, "Is that your son? I think I saw him some days ago. I haven't seen him lately though. Where's he gone?"

"He doesn't stay here. He was just here for a holiday. He stays in the US. See that's his wife, Carol," she said pointing at another photograph of a blonde lady with two kids. "She's an American. But what a lovely girl. And so traditional. And that's my grandson, Neil. He's two. And this is my granddaughter, Rita. She's just completed four," Mrs Ghose continued, pointing at the photographs and suddenly realised that she was talking to herself. "Oh dear. What a badly brought up girl the Roys have. Just like that mother of her's. Didn't even say goodbye."

Srimoti made her way home unsteadily. She locked herself in her room for the better part of the evening and cried uncontrollably. Arijit was married. He had not told her. Not that she had asked. She had assumed he was single. Just an assumption. But then why did he profess his love for her, when all along he was married? All those mushy notes and cosy evenings. He didn't mean it one bit. And to think she had believed him. Believed in his love. She had even been willing to shed her virginity for this cad. He had wanted to take her to bed, he had hinted a couple of times. And she had almost succumbed to his charms. "Bastard! He just wanted to have sex with me," Srimoti wept and in the same breath exclaimed, "Oh God! Then why do I love him so? Please God. Help me. Help me out."

Through her sobs she heard knocks on her door.

"Simu, open up. It's Ma."

Wiping her eyes, she opened the door. When she saw her mother, the dam burst. Sobbing piteously, she flung herself on her mother, "Ma, I don't know what's happening to me. I think I'm going crazy!"

Holding her close to her bosom, her mother smoothed her hair gently and asked, "What's the matter? Tell me, baby." And Srimoti told her.

An hour later, it was a different Mrs Roy who emerged from her daughter's room. The blood had drained from her face and she was white as a sheet. Her knees were trembling so badly that she had to hold on to the wall for support. "Oh my God! Oh my God! I didn't think I'd live to see this day."

Hearing the thud, Srimoti rushed out. Her mother was lying in the corridor in a faint. Running towards her, she yelled out to the family retainer, "Keshto, come quick. And call Bapi. Tell him Ma has fainted."

At her mother's bedside, Srimoti watched that loving face. Quiet and peaceful in sleep. She had been put under sedatives. She had suffered from palpitations of the heart after she had fainted that day.

Srimoti worried about her mother. She was the only genuine well-wisher she had.

Though an only child, Srimoti had never got on well with her father. He had been a provider all right. But there was nothing fatherly about his behaviour.

She must have been six or seven then. He would pinch her bottom and squeeze her nipples so hard that tears would start in her eyes. At first she complained to her wet nurse but the old lady hushed her up saying, "*Chhee chhee*. Never say such things about your father. What will people say? Nobody will believe you. They'll say you've got the devil's mind. That you cooked it up yourself."

Confused, Srimoti kept quiet. Years later she would nail down the old man in public with her acerbic comments and watch with satisfaction while he squirmed.

Her mother knew nothing of this. Srimoti was wise enough to understand that her parents did not have the best of marriages. Her father was completely in awe of his wife while she treated him with veiled contempt. These revelations would have only added to her pain.

Right then she made up her mind on one thing. "God forbid, should anything happen to Ma, I'll move out of the house. Live with anyone, anywhere. Beg, borrow, and steal. But never, never with this old fogey. I'll never share the same roof with him alone." Tears streamed down her face as she slumped back on the chair, physically and emotionally drained.

"Simu, Simu."

Srimoti woke up with a start to find her mother calling her. She hurried upto her and asked, "How are you feeling Ma? Can I get you something? Tell me."

"Nothing my child," Mrs Roy smiled wanly, "You look tired. You need some sleep. Have you eaten anything?"

"I'm not hungry," Srimoti lied.

"Why don't you go home and get some rest? I'm fine now. I'll join you soon."

"No way," Srimoti held her mother's hand firmly, "I'm not leaving you here alone. I'll go home only when the doctors discharge you. I'll take you with me."

"Silly girl," her mother smiled as she ruffled her hair. "It has been a bad day for you, hasn't it? First Arijit and then me. Poor child."

There was a pause. Neither spoke. In the hurly-burly of events in the last twenty-four hours, Arijit had slipped out of her mind completely. Now the pain and hurt came flooding back.

"Simu, I have to tell you something," Mrs Roy's soft voice broke the silence. "I don't know whether you will be able to forgive me after that, but nevertheless I have to get it off my chest. It is the truth and you must know. And I do not want you to find out from someone else."

"Ma, can't it wait till you're better?"

"No, child. Should anything happen to me, you must know this."

After a pregnant pause, her mother began, "I come from a poor but educated family. My husband was hardly educated, but rich. His family almost bribed my father to let me marry their son. Though my father knew we were not compatible, he succumbed to their wishes because he had two more daughters to marry off.

"From day one we were mismatched and very unhappy. I was eighteen and my husband, twenty-eight. For five years I waited for a child but I couldn't conceive. My husband and his relatives ridiculed me and called me barren. One day, much against his wishes, we consulted a specialist. The fault was with him. He was sterile. I was shattered. He had deliberately hidden it from me and my family before we got married. My father would never have got me married to him had he known about this. My husband made me promise not to reveal this to anyone. I did as I was told like an obedient Indian wife.

"Seven long years passed. And then I met a man—good-looking, caring, humorous, everything your father was not. He was a good ten years younger than me. But I succumbed to his charm like a schoolgirl. We had a beautiful relationship, one of the most memorable phases of my life. He was leaving for the States for higher studies when I discovered I was pregnant with his child. I told him. He suggested I abort. But I couldn't. I needed you to fill the barren space in my life.

"My husband was absolutely livid when I told him. But for once in my entire married life, I stood my ground. I was adamant. I threatened to expose his sterility if he didn't allow me to keep my baby. He called it blackmail, but the coward that he is, he kept quiet and went along with my plans.

"Then you came along Simu. Yes. You. You are that child, born out of wedlock."

"*Ma*! You mean to say..." Srimoti choked.

"Yes, Simu. And your father is Arijit Ghose."

Bhabhiji

Ek di ma andhi
Do di ma kaani
Teean di ma tikkhal
Chautha di ma rani

(The mother of one son is blind; the mother of two is blind in one eye; the mother of three is unlucky; but the mother of four is always a queen.)

An old saying in Punjab. The last line best describes Bhabhiji. Seema Bakshi's sister-in-law. As also Meenakshi Bakshi's sister-in-law. Similarly, Sunita Bakshi's. Their husband, at different points in time, Gautam Bakshi's older brother, Govind's wife Rajvinder. Or Raj for short. But best known to all and sundry as Bhabhiji. The "esteemed" Bhabhiji.

When Gautam first set eyes on Raj three decades ago, he was shocked: at thirty-one, you could hardly call her a young bride. The four front teeth of her upper jaw stuck out, in a cruel scowl. She did not blush much. Nor was she slim, like most young brides Gautam had seen. The result of sitting home idle for more than a decade, with nothing to occupy her but bits and pieces of housework. And of course, the occasional parade in front of prospective bridegrooms, dressed in heavy mock zari-cream-nylon saris and ornaments. Who came, saw, and had the odd *kaju katlis* and *chai* at the Kapoor house, never to return again. The same sari and ornaments in which she finally came as a bride to the Bakshi house.

"*Arre*, did you see Bakshiji's *bahu*?" Gautam heard his neighbour, Roop *chachiji*, ask her sister-in-law. "*Saskshat chudail*. A witch in person."

"*Chudail ayee, chudail ayee.*" Gautam heard the neighbourhood children chanting, looking towards his house. At twenty-one, he did not bother with such things. But he did notice, however, that his *bhabhi* walked with a limp. He would discover later that her feet were twisted inwards. Polio? Or was it fate? He did not give it much thought.

Govindbhai was, however, ecstatic. Over the moon. At thirty-two, Govind, apart from having remained a bachelor, was also a virgin. As far as Gautam knew, he did not have a single female admirer, leave alone have a crush on a girl. But that was Govindbhai. Shy, soft, quiet, reticent—a saint. Also, unenterprising, indifferent, slothful, lazy—a lout.

But then what was one to do? After all, he was Gautam's brother. And there was nothing the latter could do about it. So like a true sibling, he felt happy for his brother. After years he had seen Govindbhai smile. And it was Bhabhiji who was responsible for bringing that smile on his face. And he would remember that always, inspite of the childish cries of, "*chudail, chudail*".

Many months later, one afternoon, Gautam was sitting on the charpoy in the verandah with his father. Govindbhai and Bhabhiji had just left for a matinee show of *Sholay* at the cinema hall in the Chowk. "Bauji, can I ask you something?"

"*Hanh* bhai, tell me."

"Physically there is nothing wrong with Bhaisaab..."

"So?" Bauji asked.

"No. I was just wondering...I know there is nothing wrong...in fact Rajbhabhi is quite nice...but don't you think Bhaisaab deserved a more pleasant-looking wife," Gautam finally blurted out.

"Ha, ha, ha, ha," Bauji roared in mock laughter. "More pleasant-looking wife," he imitated Gautam. "*Saala woh kaamchor, haramkhor*...who do you think would have married that lazy, illiterate fool. He is over thirty and does not have a job. Nobody is foolish enough to give their daughter to this nincompoop. He has to make do with this defective *maal* from the Kapoor *khandan*," Bauji gave a sad laugh.

"This is all I could get for your brother, *beta*. At least she will be faithful to him and we will have someone to do the housework for us. After your mother's death, I have been doing the cooking and I am tired of it. At least you work in the city. Your brother sits at home and does not even help with the housework. That... he should be grateful someone has agreed to marry him. I hope he manages to feed her."

"But didn't I tell you not to have kids now? So what was the hurry, Bhaisaab?" Gautam was furious with his brother. Govind just looked down, shamefacedly. It had been a year since Bauji's death and almost two years since Bhaisaab had got married. Nearly a year after their marriage, Bhabhiji bore Bhaisaab a *hatta katta puttar*, a healthy son. They named him Johnny, after the comedian Johnny Walker. Bauji, inspite of being happy at becoming a grandfather, was nevertheless a little upset.

"*Kya jaldi thi bachcha paida karne ki?* What was the hurry? *Naukri to hai nahin...*" Bauji had admonished his son.

That was over a year ago. And with Bauji no more, it was Gautam's turn to play father to Bhaisaab. It was he who had been supporting his brother's family for the past two years. Both he and Bauji had explained to Govind and his wife the necessity of not having any more children, since Govind was unemployed. "It is not easy to bring up children these days. Things are so expensive, Bhaisaab." Gautam had tried to reason.

"One son is more than enough. *Ab, nasbandi karwa lo,*" Bauji had added. Bhaisaab seemed embarrassed, while

Bhabhiji looked upset. At the end, both remained indifferent.

The result, another son, following closely a year after the first one. They named him Jeetu, after the evergreen Bollywood hero, Jeetendra.

"Just what do the two of you take me for? A money-making machine? I slog while you f...?" Gautam was livid when his brother called up to tell him that he had become an uncle for the third time. As usual, his rants fell on deaf ears.

"Listen carefully, Bhaisaab. This is the last time I am warning you. One more baby and I will stop sending you money. You can fend for yourself and your family."

Gautam's third nephew was called Jackie, after an upcoming young Bollywood hero, Jackie Shroff.

The next few years were uneventful for the Bakshis. Bhabhiji did not conceive and Gautam was relieved. Thank God! No more new mouths to feed.

"*Arre, arre, hat hat,*" the nattily dressed Gautam yelled, trying to fob off the street urchins as he wended his way towards his brother's house in Dehrawalla Galli in Ludhiana. It was almost a decade since he had been there. Much had changed. It was difficult to recognise the area.

"*Arre, sun bachche.* Come here," he gestured to one of the urchins playing. A boy, about nine years old, in a torn dirty *banyan* and *chaddis* walked upto him, looking suspicious, but curious. His face and nails were black with grime and there was snot running from his nose. Two boys of similar appearance tagged after him.

"Can you show me Govind Bakshi's house?" Gautam asked.

The three boys giggled and then started running. One of them gestured to Gautam to follow them. Gautam obeyed. On reaching the house, one of them ran in screaming, "Mummy, Mummy. There's a smart-looking man at the door asking for Daddy."

Gautam almost collapsed when he realised that the little boys that he had taken for street urchins were actually his nephews. They must be Johnny, Jeetu and Jackie, he thought to himself.

Later in the evening, Gautam sat down nursing a drink, trying to get over the shock of seeing his nephews. It was then that he noticed Bhabhiji gently rocking a baby in the *jhula*, while simultaneously attending to other chores. It was almost eight years since his last nephew had been born. Bhabhiji must be in her forties now, Gautam absentmindedly thought to himself.

"*Arre* Bhabhiji, whose baby are you minding? The neighbour's?" Gautam asked jokingly. Both Bhaisaab and Bhabhiji smiled sheepishly.

"It is ours," Bhabhiji said softly.

"No. You are joking," Gautam exploded.

Bhaisaab and Bhabhiji remained silent.

"How could you?" Gautam was livid. "You guys will never learn. And look at your age. You are hardly getting any younger, you know?"

"We know," Bhabhiji said. "But we always wanted a little girl. So we thought we might give it one last try..."

This woman is impossible, Gautam thought. Always ready with an excuse.

Whatever you may think Devarji, Bhabhiji thought to herself, from now on I am the queen of my destiny. The mother of four sons—a rani in the true sense of the word.

Seema first met her future husband at a friend's house. Their common friend Ratin. It was Ratin's birthday and he introduced them to each other. It was obvious to everybody present that they made a good pair.

Both were footloose and fancy-free and over a couple of Bacardis, they exchanged phone numbers. What followed were two months of an intense, as they say, whirlwind romance before they decided to tie the knot. Gautam was nearing forty when he decided to get married and he was keen his brother and his family—the only family he had—be present. So he called them from Ludhiana. Seema wanted a simple court marriage.

The registration was a low-key affair, with select friends in attendance. Later, Gautam took Seema home. Jackie answered the doorbell.

"Where is Mummy?" Gautam asked.

"In the kitchen," Jackie replied in an obvious hurry. Turning his back on them, he ran inside, yelling, "She is cooking dinner."

"*Arre*, come here. Come and meet your new *chachi*. Seema, this is Bhaisaab's third son, Jackie."

"Hello, Aunty," and within seconds Jackie had vanished again.

"Must be busy with his homework," Gautam tried by way of an explanation. "Come, let's go in and meet the rest of the family."

"Hello, children. This is your new *chachi*. Say hello." Gautam told his nephews, huddling around a carom board.

Without bothering to get up, they just turned around, said a perfunctory "hello" and resumed their game. A little taken aback, but pretending not to notice it, Gautam took his new bride to meet his brother, who was glued to the television at the other end of the room.

"Bhaisaab. *Aiye. Miliye*. This is Seema, my wife. I told you we were getting married today. Well, we have got married." Then turning to Seema, he said, "Seema, this is my elder brother, Govind bhaisaab."

Seema bowed to touch his feet in obeisance, but Bhaisaab continued to sit. He merely bent forward a little, muttered a sullen, "*Bas, bas. Jeete raho,*" and went back to the serial he was watching.

Seema felt a little hurt. When she turned towards Govind, the latter tried to cover up his embarrassment by almost dragging his bride towards the kitchen. "Let us go and meet Bhabhiji."

"I don't think any of your family members are keen to meet me," Seema protested. Govind pretended not to hear as he led her towards the kitchen.

"*Arre* Bhabhiji. Come. Meet your new *bahu*. This is Seema, my wife. Seema, this is my bhabhi." Bhabhiji continued to cook while Seema bent down to touch her feet. Bhabhiji moved a little awkwardly and said, "It is alright. What would you like to have? Some tea? Or a cold drink?"

"Imagine the cheek of that bitch? Bhabhiji actually asked me whether I wanted tea or a cold drink, as if I were a guest. In my own house? Was that any way to welcome a new bride? Especially after all that Gautam has done for her and her family?" Seema said as she sipped her coffee.

"That bitch did not even give me any *shagun*," Meenakshi joined in. "Not even a rupee or a coconut. And imagine Gautam trying to stand up for her by saying, 'Oh, you should not take it so seriously. *Bechari* doesn't have any money.' *Bechari*, my left foot. Especially after living off my husband's largesse for so long."

It was almost eight years since Seema and Gautam had divorced. In fact, the day Seema had entered Gautam's house as a bride, she realised that she had entered the wrong house. Her decision to marry Gautam Bakshi was all wrong. Putting up with the indifference of his family members was one thing, but Gautam trying to cover up for them was another matter altogether.

"I thought you said your brother and his family stayed in Punjab?" she had questioned Gautam later.

"Yes, they do. But I had wanted them to meet you," Gautam had admitted sheepishly. "Besides...."

"Besides, what?" Seema asked.

"Besides, you know the terrorist problem in Punjab...things are quite messy out there....I thought it would be better if they stayed here with me..."

Seema would have none of it. Independent by nature, she felt Gautam's inquisitive relatives had invaded her privacy in every way, apart from the fact that Bhabhiji tried to rule their lives with her subtle ways. Needless to say, the marriage did not last more than six months. Two years later, when the divorce came through, Gautam felt sad. And lonely. Sad, because he had lost Seema. Lonely, because, inspite of being surrounded by his relatives, he had nothing in common with them. He was a lonely man at forty.

Three years after his divorce, Gautam decided to take the plunge again. This time with his long-time colleague,

Meenakshi—a dusky, doe-eyed Tamilian beauty with long, lustrous hair. But, of course, both were cautious this time. Gautam realised that if he wanted a hassle-free married life, he would have to get his brother's family off his back. They could not share the same roof with him and his wife. His scheming Bhabhiji, his lazy brother, and the bunch of ill-mannered, unkempt nephews. So he rented a tiny, one-bedroom apartment nearby and told Bhaisaab and family to shift. Bhabhiji initially protested, feigning mock concern for Gautam, but ultimately relented. Like his other colleagues at work, Meenakshi knew the reason for his break-up with Seema. So she bade her time till Gautam's brother's family was out of his house for good.

"You were lucky not to have those scruffy nephews and that pest of a Bhabhiji around," Seema said as she took another sip of her coffee. "You know she never used to bathe for days on end. And every time she hugged me, her body odour and the smell of sweat would drive me mad."

"What do you mean lucky?" Meenakshi said indignantly as she bit into her muffin, "Their absence was as good as their presence."

"Hey, don't play with words. What do you mean?"

"You know, Gautam rented an apartment for them which was barely ten minutes away from our house. Every day, on some pretext, the family would land up at my door. One day it was Bhabhiji who wanted to make *pakodi kadhi* for her dear devarji. And she never forgot to remind me how much he missed Punjabi food and did not like *idli-dosa*. It was all a lot of bull," Meenakshi fumed.

Seema giggled.

"It is not as funny as you think," Meenakshi said, but could not help smiling. "Very often the entire family would turn up in the morning and on most days not leave past midnight. The brother would lie around like a sloth bear, watching the most inane programmes on TV, while those brats would make an awful ruckus. The living room resembled a railway platform, with half a dozen bodies sprawled around throughout the day. You know, I used to feel embarrassed to have guests over. And if a friend happened to drop in, I had no choice but to take her to my bedroom. Imagine being restricted in my own house."

"I can imagine. I have been through all this myself," Seema said.

"I wish you had warned me," Meenakshi said.

"Well... had you asked me..."

"Ah well...if only...Anyway it is too late for that now. The divorce should come through by next month. Thank God we did not have any kids, though Gautam was keen on having children. Just imagine, they would have had to go through all this. It can be very upsetting for children," Meenakshi said.

"Well, as long as his Bhabhiji is around, I doubt if Gautam will be able to have a settled married life. That woman...she hates to see him happy. As long as he remains a bachelor, her sons have a claim on his property, you see. Anyway, they are up to no good—as lazy and useless as that father of theirs. It's disgusting the way that man eats, with his mouth open. And he would make such a racket that the neighbourhood would come to know that he was eating. Chomp, chomp, chomp," Seema said. The girls giggled, "And worse still, he would leave his dirty plates for me to wash. Lout!"

"I must tell you something, Seema," Meenakshi said, "A few days after our wedding, Bhabhiji told me quietly, 'Listen beta, now that you have come, I can die in peace. My children are like your children. You need not take the trouble of having any.' The nerve of that woman. Mothering those unwashed, rowdy brats, what an idea."

"Whenever you need money, you think of me. After all that I have done for you, is this the way to treat me? You should have taken my opinion on the matter. After all I am your financial provider." Gautam was yelling at his brother and bhabhi. Sunita, his third wife, hovered at a distance, hoping that this uncomfortable situation would end soon. The matter under discussion was Bhaisaab and Bhabhiji's eldest son, Johnny's impending marriage.

"You know Johnny is not earning enough. What is two thousand rupees these days? How is he going to support his wife?" Gautam was upset. "And don't think I can help financially. All my life I have supported you, Bhaisaab, your wife and children. Now I need to take it easy. And it is time you told your sons to start fending for themselves. Tell them not to depend on Uncle, because Uncle is exhausted."

Much against Gautam's wishes, Johnny married Sandra, a girl from the same church that Bhabhiji attended. Another reason for Gautam's anger at his bhabhi was her recent conversion to a born-again Christian sect. He did not give a damn about her, but what upset him was the fact that his brother and nephews also followed suit. And he was more upset that his nephews were being forced into marriage with these born-again Christian girls.

A few months after Johnny's marriage, Jeetu and Jackie both decided to marry too. Sally and Radha went to the same church but unlike Sandra, they were not Bhabhiji's choices. The boys had decided on the girls themselves. Though Jeetu worked in a canteen with a shipping firm and earned a paltry five hundred rupees more than Johnny, Jackie was still happily unemployed. Besides, another young Bakshi was waiting in the wings—Jai, who squandered his college fees watching Hindi films. Though he was not named after any film actor, unlike his older siblings, the film bug had bitten Jai and he secretly aspired to become a Bollywood actor. This inspite of his buck teeth, which he had inherited from his mother, and a ninety-five kilogramme frame.

"Gautam, this is simply getting out of hand. You just cannot allow your brother and bhabhi to take advantage of you like this," Sunita told her husband after Govind and his wife had left.

"But what could I have done? Throw them out of the house? After all, he is my brother. My only blood relative."

"I know and all he does is take advantage of you. You should have been firm. Imagine Jeetu and Jackie getting married. They are not even settled. How will they support their wives?" Sunita asked.

"It is their problem," Gautam answered.

"It's your problem as well. They will keep coming back to you, begging their dear uncle for help. Just like Johnny, you will end up supporting their wives and kids too. And your brother and bhabhi will be enjoying all the *tamasha*."

"Alright, alright. Mind your own business," Gautam snapped at Sunita.

"It is my business too," Sunita snapped back at her husband. "You cannot buy me a car which I need and you dole out money to celebrate the weddings of your good-for-nothing nephews. A lac of rupees each! My God! I wish

I were your nephew instead of your wife. All you gave me when we married was a thin *mangalsutra* and a plain wedding band."

"Oh, shut up. You know you live like a queen. Look at my brother's family. They live so miserably."

"But that is their own doing. You bought them a house bigger than our flat and they keep it like a pig sty. Thanks to your Bhabhiji. She has no sense of hygiene, doesn't bathe for days herself. How is she going to keep a clean house?"

"Now enough is enough. Don't go on and on," Gautam said.

"But why not?" Sunita asked in defiance.

"Because whatever it is, they are my family and I don't want you to criticise them."

"I see. So I mean nothing to you. You know, Seema and Meenu were right. As long as your nephews and Bhabhiji are around scheming, you will never be able to have a family life of your own."

"So you have been meeting those women on the sly? Why don't you go and join them?" Gautam said to his wife.

"I will soon enough. And let me tell you, both of them are so much happier without you. Which woman would want such a lot of baggage, along with a husband..."

Stung, Gautam let loose a string of abuses. "Enough. I've had enough of this."

Muttering to herself, Sunita swept out of the room.

It was Christmas and Gautam was lonely, inspite of his house being full of people. Sunita had left; both of them had been undergoing a trial separation for the past four months.

Bhabhiji insisted on celebrating Christmas with her family at her brother-in-law's house because, she claimed, she wanted to alleviate his loneliness. This, inspite of Gautam insisting that he wanted to be left alone. Finally, he had to give in to her persuasion. The recent developments had pleased Bhabhiji no end. Once again, she was the unchallenged matron of her brother-in-law's house.

She was busy instructing her *bahus* and delegating work to them. The menu was chicken curry and vegetable pulao. Sally, Jeetu's wife, a Goan, had been given the duty of making chicken vindaloo, which was her specialty. Radha, Jackie's wife, was busy making preparations for the pulao while Sandra, the eldest *bahu*, peeled and cut vegetables. The three brothers played cards and sipped their beers. Jai was baby-sitting his young nephews and nieces. Bhaisaab, Bhabhiji and Gautam sat in one corner of the room, the brothers drinking in silence. In between, Bhabhiji kept limping to and from the kitchen with her instructions. She loved such moments when she oversaw everything herself, especially in her brother-in-law's house. She felt like a queen. A rani.

Gautam, bored, started counting the family members. Brother, bhabi, four nephews, three wives, two children...eleven members, excluding him. A football team. Gautam smiled to himself. No wonder Sunita used to refer to his family as a football team. Gosh, I have actually raised a football team in all these years, he thought wryly. I deserve credit for this.

"Marry Christmas, Uncle," Sandra handed a plate of *pakodas* to Gautam.

"Merry Christmas," Gautam replied, jolted out of his reverie. "Oh, thank you," he said looking at the plate. "You made it?"

"Well...yes...Both Radha and me."

Gautam knew that it was Radha who must have made it, but Sandra always liked to take credit for everything. Sandra Gill was a born-again Christian *jat* from Ludhiana, who came from a very poor family. She was beautiful in a rustic sort of way and it was Bhabhiji who, during one of her visits to Ludhiana, had chosen the girl for her favourite son, Johnny.

"She is a poor and simple girl. Just right for the family. Very hardworking and loves nursing and caring for people," she tried to convince Gautam about the wisdom of her choice. That was before the marriage. What happened after marriage was another story. Sandra was anything but hardworking. She loved to laze around throughout the day, watching television and gossiping with the neighbourhood ladies. When her daughter was born, she made her father-in-law look after the child while her mother-in-law managed the household. Since Bhabhiji herself had selected Sandra, she could hardly complain. Serves her right for trying to rush poor Johnny into marriage, Gautam thought to himself.

"Uncle," Sandra smiled as she sat herself next to Gautam. "I wanted to say something."

"Yes. Go on," Gautam said.

"Well... er... how do I start. It is like this. Johnny and me are finding it difficult to stay in the same house with the rest of the family. Now that Jeetu and Jackie are married, there is very little privacy."

"So?"

"We thought of shifting. Going in for a one-bedroom-hall-kitchen flat."

"So? Who is stopping you?"

"We don't have the money. So we thought if you could..."

"When you have the money start looking for a place," Gautam cut her short. "Jeetu, come here beta," he turned towards his nephew, "make me a small drink please."

Snubbed, Sandra got up and left. The cheek of the girl to come and ask me so point blank, Gautam thought. She has no *tameez*...no manners. After all, she is only a daughter-in-law.

After a while Sally came in. "Dinner is ready," she announced. "Come, let us all eat."

Then turning to Gautam she asked, "How's your drink, Uncle? Shall I get you another one?"

"No, thank you *bete*. I will have dinner now." Gautam said, a little taken aback by Sally's sudden friendliness. In fact, she had always seemed a little shy. So unlike Sandra. Maybe her school job is doing her some good—she is opening up.

"When's school reopening?" Gautam asked.

"Jan 15th," Sally said.

"Are you both planning to take Tushar somewhere during the holidays? To your mother's—Goa? It must be lovely out there at this time of the year?"

"Yes, it is, Uncle. We wanted to go but there is no money," Sally said.

Oh God! Not again. The Bakshis never seem to have enough money. All their monetary problems seem to surface when they see me, Gautam thought, with a sense of wonderment. He tried to look the other way. Sally waited for a while, trying to gauge his mood. She was not as brazen as her older sister-in-law. In fact, she was wondering whether she should broach the topic of a monetary loan from Uncle at all. He did not seem very forthcoming. She had also warned Jeetu that it would not be fair on Uncle, considering he himself was going through a financial crunch, what with an impending divorce.

But then Jeetu was just like the rest of his family. They loved to live off their uncle, like a bunch of parasites. They never gave a thought to Gautam Uncle's physical or mental well-being. All they could think of was money, money and more money. At least that is how they had been tutored by their mother. Just squeeze him dry. After all, your father is his only brother and you boys are his only blood relations—*aapka hak banta hai*. It is your birthright. No wonder all the brothers including her husband were good-for-nothing, lazy bums. Most of the time they were out of jobs and their idea of constructive work was playing cards and having beer.

When Sally had first met Jeetu, she was quite impressed by his rustic good looks. Unlike her older sister-in-law, Sandra, she came from a well-to-do middle class family. Jeetu had pursued her relentlessly for more than a year before she gave in to his persuasions. Initially her parents had opposed the match because they thought Jeetu Bakshi was a wastrel. But Jeetu seemed sincere in his love for Sally and promised his future in-laws that he would do his best after marriage.

Jeetu kept part of his promise though. He got himself a ground job with a shipping company in Powai as a cook but did not do much beyond it. He was not too keen on doing any better and therefore did not put in that extra effort in his workplace. From time to time he would keep borrowing money from his uncle under some pretext or the other and never bothered paying back. Not that Gautam harboured any expectations of getting back the money he lent his brother or his nephews. Initially Sally found the whole exercise embarrassing. But when she realised that everybody was sponging off Gautam Uncle, she relented and fell into line.

"Jeetu has got an offer to start a snacks counter in Bhawan's College," Sally finally spoke.

"Good. That is good news," Gautam replied disinterestedly.

"But there is a little problem, Uncle," Sally said a little sheepishly.

There was an awkward silence. Finally Gautam said, "Yes. What is it now?"

"The authorities want an initial deposit of three lac rupees," Sally said.

"Well, that is a lot of money," Gautam said.

"Exactly Uncle. And we cannot afford it. So we thought if you could lend us the sum..."

"Forget it," Gautam snapped. "I don't have that kind of money to throw away."

"But Uncle, it is for our future. It will settle us for life."

"Listen, my girl. You are more sensible than the others. So don't waste your time in such useless talk. You know and I know, that that husband of yours is as lazy as the rest of his family. He barely puts in eight hours in his job—you think he is going to slog round the clock. After all, a business is more difficult to sustain than a nine-to-five job. None of these boys have any enterprise in them. So no point in wasting your time and mine on this. End of subject. Anything more?"

Sally kept her eyes on the floor. I should not have asked in the first place, she thought. Imagine having to hear all this because of Jeetu. And I had warned him against asking anything from Uncle.

"Sorry, Uncle," Sally muttered softly.

"It's alright, beta. I don't mind helping out, but only when someone really deserves it. At the moment I don't think any of the Bakshi boys deserve my help or sympathy."

"I understand, Uncle," Sally nodded and quietly walked away.

As soon as Sally had left, with a growing sense of apprehension, Gautam saw Radha walking towards him.

The youngest *bahu* was a rather quiet girl and kept to herself. But news had already filtered to Gautam that she did not get along with her mother-in-law. Obviously, thought Gautam to himself. Having a mother-in-law in these modern times is curse enough, without having to endure one like Bhabhiji. Gautam had also heard that Sandra and Bhabhiji conspired to make life miserable for Radha. The latter's parents had migrated from the Punjab to Canada recently for better prospects. And since both Sandra and Bhabhiji knew that Radha had no one to turn to, they really bullied the poor girl.

But then it was none of his business and there was nothing he could do about it. Not that he wanted to. His family never shared their good times with him. It was only in times of trouble that they kept coming back to him.

Radha was animatedly talking to someone on the cell phone as she came towards Gautam. It was one of those flashy handsets and belonged to Jackie. The bum doesn't even have a steady job and look how he flashes his mobile around, Gautam smiled.

"Uncle, Papa is calling from Caynaydda. He wants to wish you Marry Christmas," Radha said as she handed the handset to Gautam.

"Hello Sir, a very merry Christmas to you and all at home. It must be very cold out there?"

"*Hanh* Bhaisaab, it is quite cold heer," Ravi Chedhda spoke with his newly acquired accent. "How is everything there?"

"All's well," Gautam replied. "When are you coming over?"

"*Ab kya bataoon*, Bhaisaab. You know everything. Life is very tough out heer. We are still illegal immigrants. We can barely make ends meet, where will we get the money to visit India."

"Yes...yes...I see..." Gautam muttered something inaudibly.

"Gautambhai, you are like my younger brother. I wanted to share something with you," Radha's father said after a slight pause.

"Yes. Tell me."

"I don't know how to say it....You see it is like this. My daughter is not happy in her *sasural*. Your Bhabhiji is quite rude to her. I don't blame your bhabhi for this. It is basically Sandra's fault. She does not get along with Radha because my daughter does not give in to her bullying. As a result, she has poisoned Bhabhiji's mind against my daughter and she is mistreated in the house."

"I see," Gautam said. Nothing surprising, he thought to himself.

"Bhaisaab, you know we stay so far away from our daughter. My wife and me always worry about her. So we thought if we could bring her over heer. Both Jackie and Radha could come and settle heer with us and they can earn well heer..."

"But, you just said that you were illegal immigrants yourselves ... how can you take on their responsibility."

"Oh, you don't worry about that. We have sources. We will organise everything. There will be no problem. They just need to come heer."

"So why don't you call them there. Anyway, Jackie is hardly doing much here."

"I know," Radha's father replied. "But you see, I do not have the money for their airfare heer. If you could pay for their tickets, then..."

It took a minute for the request to register. Then Gautam snapped at him. "Listen Bhaisaab...someone must have misinformed you, but I do not have that kind of money to spare."

"No, no. I did not mean that. I was just looking for my daughter's happiness. After all she is your daughter now," Radha's father added.

"Sorry, but you can keep your daughter to yourself. I do not want any responsibilities or any daughters. Please understand that. And Merry Christmas," he said firmly. Then turning to Radha he handed her the phone, "Here take this. Talk to your father."

Radha figured something must have gone wrong from the tone of Uncle's voice, so she quickly left the room.

As if one Bhabhiji was not enough. Now I have three more to contend with. All *bhabhijis* in the making, Gautam thought as he sipped the remnants of his drink. Enough is enough. Now I am going to put a stop to all this.

With a mix of surprise and relief, he suddenly realised that he no longer cared. Gone was that feeling of responsibility towards his elder brother that had dogged him after his father's death and throughout his three marriages.

"*Devarji, khana lagaye?* Shall we lay the table?"

It was Bhabhiji.

Pages from Indulata Debi's Diary

(Loosely based on the memoirs of Haimabati Ghosh, one of the first women doctors in Bengal)

March 1896

I have just succeeded Sushila Debi as the head doctor of the Hooghly Dufferin Women's Hospital for female patients in Chinsurah. Sushiladi was the first Bengali "lady doctor" in charge of the hospital and was a year senior to me in Campbell Medical College. She resigned within a month of her appointment citing reasons of dissatisfaction with the doctor's quarters. My starting salary is rupees forty per month and I have two young men helping me out; one as a dresser (nurse) and the other as a compounder (pharmacist). The hospital can accommodate upto thirty patients.

In the early years of the nineteenth century, Prasun Chandra Sen Chaudhuri, a *zamindar* from Khulna (now in

Bangladesh), fought British indigo planters who had come to destroy the land of the poor peasants in Bengal. Fighting alongside the peasants and against the British, the Sen Chaudhuris incurred heavy financial losses. This, coupled with the traditional aristocratic vices of drinking and womanising, depleted the Sen Chaudhuris' fortunes.

Amidst these conditions in 1870, Indulata Sen Chaudhuri was born to Pratap Chandra, son of Prasun Chandra, and his wife, Lajjabati Debi. Indu's mother was disappointed with her birth as she had wanted a son. But Pratap Chandra was overjoyed. He ordered for celebratory music to be played and distributed sweets and money amongst his subjects.

"My daughter will equal a hundred sons. The times are changing Indu's ma, men and women will soon be equal. Stop mourning the birth of your daughter. Take my word, she will do you proud one day," Pratap told Lajjabati.

He pampered Indu no end and often dressed her as a boy, much to her mother's chagrin. He fondly nicknamed her Khukibabu or Mr Girl. Indu was a tomboy and mostly played with her male cousins. Pratap Chandra encouraged her to study and Indu started taking lessons along with the boys of the house. It was soon evident to everyone that Indu was an extraordinary student—eager, sharp.

The women in the family, Indu's mother, grandmother and aunts were against her education, believing firmly that the fate awaiting an educated girl was early widowhood.

But Pratap Chandra would have none of this. He had great plans for his daughter. "She will be the first woman graduate from Khulna. Just you wait," he would boast.

However, fate had other plans in store for Indu. When she was eight, her father died of a sudden heart attack. He was found dead in the room of Anguribai, his favourite nautch girl, in one of the notorious areas of the town. Not so much his tragic death, but its circumstances, filled his young widow with shame, hurt and anger.

With her husband gone, the only person she could vent her emotions on was her daughter, the sign of their union, the apple of Pratap Chandra's eye when he lived. Her behaviour towards Indu changed. She grew harsh, often cursing her for being her father's daughter. Aided and abetted by Indu's grandmother and other women in the family, Lajjabati arranged Indu's marriage when the latter was barely nine. Though most girls in those days married between the ages of twelve and fourteen, Indu was married off much earlier, against her wishes. The groom was Satish Chandra Ghosh, a twice-widowed forty-eight-year-old man with a son and a daughter older than Indu.

An early marriage did not always mean an immediate consummation and often the girl returned to her parents, to be sent back when she was physically and emotionally mature. Indu, however, stayed on with her husband. His attempts to consummate the marriage, most often in a drunken state, were nightmares. She was repelled by the ways he forcefully undressed her, fondled her roughly and tried to invade her private parts. Her cries would put him off and often these little trysts ended in resounding slaps on her face.

"Why did I marry you? To pickle and preserve you in a jar?" Satish would yell viciously while Indu sobbed piteously.

Hurt and humiliated, Indu had no one to share her thoughts with. Neither her mother-in-law nor her sisters-in-law took kindly to her, as they thought her pampered upbringing and education had spoilt her.

Barely a year after her marriage, Indu was widowed. Satish died of cirrhosis of the liver. Their marriage was unconsummated.

September 1896

In the past six months we have served a total of 112 inpatients, 1,124 outpatients and performed 14 major and 48 minor operations. I think this hospital is likely to prove very beneficial to the residents of the districts.

Dr Badrinath Mukherji, who is my supervising surgeon, keeps staring at me and talking to me suggestively about venereal diseases. When I complained to the civil surgeon Dr Biswajit Sen about Dr Mukherji's indecent behaviour, Dr Sen told the latter to behave himself. Dr Mukherji was highly affronted. Last night on my way home he set his henchmen Gopal and Tulu on me. However, I managed to escape with only a bruised arm. I will not be cowed down by such threats.

Though the Dufferin Fund advocates medical care for women by women, the presence of these two men in this hospital completely violates this rule. But the elite women are more concerned about sharing the same ward with women from poorer segments rather than the presence of the male staff. When a woman of elite status needs medical care, I normally make house calls or put them up in my quarters (if the case is of a more serious nature). I don't care what people say behind my back but my mission is to provide women with medical care, not transform the social system.

Soon after, Indu lost her mother and then her mother-in-law. Her stay at her in-laws' became increasingly difficult. She found herself at loggerheads with her brothers-in-law over family property. Her sisters-in-law also felt threatened by her presence—the young widow had blossomed into an attractive and highly desirable woman.

It was then that Satish's younger brother, Pritish, took it upon himself to be Indu's protector. This was done more to gratify his sexual desires than out of any genuine concern for her well-being. Gradually Pritish succeeded where his late brother had failed. Initially Indu tried to ward off his advances, but her youthful needs got the better of her and she finally submitted to him.

While Satish's mere presence used to repulse her, she actually enjoyed being with Pritish. She began looking forward to their little meetings. Along with her diffidence she shed her inhibitions, much to Pritish's pleasant surprise.

These meetings of pleasure were soon to end. One day Pritish's wife, Bindurani, caught them red-handed. She had always had her suspicions of Indu. To avoid embarrassment within the family, it was decided that Indu would be sent to Benaras, the refuge of widows. Pritish Chandra promised to send her money every month for her upkeep. On that note Indulata left for Benaras.

October 1899

I am happy to note that over the years the Dufferin Women's Hospital has become more popular than the Victoria Zenana Hospital in Calcutta. Being the only female medical practitioner in the district, I am given a lot of love and respect from both men and women. This is also because I respect both the traditional ayurvedic medicines practised by the hakims and the kavirajes along with allopathic medicines. I have also begun experimenting with homoeopathic medicines. This branch of medicine, founded by Dr Hannemann of Germany, seems to be gaining in popularity of late. Since the medication is milder than that of allopathy, on and off I include some of these in my prescriptions. I especially favour Arnica Mont for pain relief instead of the strong allopathic painkillers.

My private house visits have increased and I have a steady and loyal group of private patients. My private income is three times more than my government salary, which is eighty rupees per month. Inspite of my name and goodwill, my male colleagues continue to harass me, with sexual innuendos and advances. They probably cannot digest the fact that a woman is doing better than most of them.

On August 21st this year, I had my second child, a daughter. Kartick and I have decided to name her Krishnakali on account of her darkish complexion. She is a pretty and healthy child.

It was a difficult birth as I am nearing thirty now. But a month after her birth, I rejoined service, though instead of the full ten hours, I work only four hours. I also have a private practice in the house. This consideration the authorities have bestowed on me under what they term as "maternity benefits".

In another four to six months' time, once Krishnakali starts taking semi-solid food and I also manage to wean her away from the breast, I will resume full duty. I have also hired a young girl, Bela, who is extremely patient with the baby. Even then I will come home every few hours in order to check up on her. After losing Keshub, I have become over-protective towards Krishnakali.

The thought of Keshub's death still haunts me. The thought that I couldn't save my baby from cholera because I was tending to other patients unsettles me. Keshub was only six months old. I will see to it that this is not repeated.

Indu was all of seventeen when she reached Benaras. Inspite of her widow's whites and shaven head, she was an attractive young woman, and men feasted their eyes on her.

The first few weeks in Benaras was spent at a cousin's place. But when her cousin's wife realised the potential

PAGES FROM INDULATA DEBI'S DIARY

threat to their marriage, she was forced to shift to an ashram for widows. Life in those ashrams was difficult—it was more like living death. The widows had to tonsure their heads, wear only a white cloth of the coarsest fabric so as not to attract male attention, and eat frugal vegetarian meals without spices, so as not to arouse their sexual desires. They prayed all day and were not allowed to leave the ashram without permission and unescorted.

Indu could not bear it for very long. She moved out and rented a small room close to the nautch girls' *gulli* in the city, all that she could afford with her meagre funds. After the first few months, money stopped coming from Pritish Chandra. In order to make ends meet, Indu had to find some form of employment. Luckily she was hired as a teacher in a small vernacular school for girls.

In those days, these types of schools—established by Indian reformist leaders—had mushroomed. Supported by local donations and run by elderly brahmin men, they offered an alternative to missionary education. Indu was hired as a teacher in such a school.

The headmaster of the school was a man called Hemendra Kishore Bandopadhyay or Banerjee (as the British had shortened it). Hembabu was in his late fifties and had two married daughters and a son. He lived with his wife and son's family near the school premises. But this did not prevent him from making passes at Indu. The young widow was initially shocked and disgusted—a toothless, emaciated old man, old enough to be her father! But there was no other way to keep body and soul together in this strange city. Indu eventually gave in.

At the mercy of lecherous men, the butt of gossip in a new city, struggling with an alien language and culture—Indu decided to go to Calcutta. From what she had heard, the British capital of India, which was liberal towards its women, would have more to offer her. There were "homes" in Calcutta where widows could live and study and even work.

She had been through so much in her twenty years. Robbed of her innocence early in life, she did not want to spend the rest of her life mourning her past and awaiting death.

Determined to make the most of her remaining years, Indu made her way to Calcutta. With whatever little she had saved, she managed to procure a rail pass. Dressed as a mendicant to avoid unwelcome attention, Indulata Ghosh entered the city of her dreams.

April 1905
Much has happened in the past few years and my busy schedule as a doctor, wife and mother have taken their toll on my health. As a "lady doctor", I have assisted in several major and minor operations, mainly removing placentas, obstructing labour, doing turnings in deliveries, opening boils and abscesses, removing warts, extracting teeth

and bandaging simple fractures. Though we were competent enough, we normally assisted male doctors in "major" surgeries. On our own we were only allowed to perform simple, relief-producing tasks. What did occasionally surprise me was the radical procedures and experiments European male doctors liked to perform on Indian patients. They regarded Indian female patients as expendable and were disappointed when women refused ovariotomies which were almost always fatal.

I know that Kartick—my "educated" and "enlightened" husband—is jealous of my professional success. He spends a lot of time doing social work for the Samaj and his financial contribution to the house is nil. Not that I mind, but what is annoying is that he expects me to take care of all the household chores even after a hard day's work. He hardly takes interest in the education of our children, Krishmakali, now six and Kundan, four, though he is at home most of the day. I have to hand over my entire earnings to him and at times when I ask for money to buy a much needed item, like a new saree or a pair of shoes, I am refused.

Kartick hates the fact that I am financially independent and controls my finances. He hates to see me well-dressed and says that it will arouse the lust of my male colleagues. He is just being petty and jealous. I have heard him gossip about me to relatives and neighbours. But I must admit that I do take satisfaction in disobeying him from time to time, modest attempts at rebellion. I don't reveal the exact amount of my earnings from my private patients to him. I keep a little for myself. I don't feel guilty at all but rather justified in doing so.

In the last six years, much against my wishes, I have endured five pregnancies, out of which four have been miscarriages, mainly *due to exhaustion and anaemia. Only the one in 1901 culminated in the birth of my son Kundan.*

One autumn afternoon in 1890, twenty-year-old Indulata arrived in Calcutta. Armed with letters of introduction written by "gentlemen of Benaras", Indu met Durgamohan Das and Shibnath Shastri, two of the stalwarts of the Sadharan Brahmo Samaj.

The Brahmo movement was a reformist movement supported by the educated elite in early nineteenth century Bengal. Its founder, Rammohun Roy, advocated social reform and widow remarriage, denounced the *sati* system and shunned idol worship and rituals which were integral to the Hindu religion. He founded the Brahmo Samaj, a reformed version of Hinduism as defined in the ancient texts of the Vedas and the Upanishads. To grant women their dignity as human beings was one of the causes of the Brahmos. To this end, they spoke for women's education, opposed early marriages and *sati* and encouraged the re-marriage of widows.

Indu's battle for survival in Calcutta had begun. In exchange for food and shelter, she took to working in different households. All along she refused marriage proposals from elderly Brahmo widowers with children, as she realised that all they wanted was a housekeeper rather than a mate. But an unpartnered adult woman, brimming with youth and beauty, was considered a hazard in those days. Indu finally gave in to the pressures from the Samaj elders and agreed to marry for a second time.

Kartick Chandra Sen was a Brahmo missionary in his mid-thirties from Midnapore and the manager of the Mission Press. Other widows considered him "too dark" to marry. The two set up house in Calcutta. Soon after their marriage, Kartick left to work for famine victims in Bihar and Indu became a boarder in one of the many private schools for girls.

At school, she met a number of Brahmo widows in Calcutta, living with their families and pursuing their studies. She was particularly impressed by the young women attending medical school and slowly started considering the study of medicine as a possible option. In 1887, the Directorate of Public Instruction had set up the Campbell Medical School and had started a three-year course for women, a new experiment in medical education. Indu was more determined than ever to continue her education now.

It was mainly due to the efforts of Sir A W Croft, the Director of Public Instructions in Bengal, that vernacular medical classes for women were started in Campbell. In 1884, Kadambini Ganguly, a Bengali Brahmo from an elite family became the first woman to be admitted to Calcutta Medical College. But the course it offered was in English and few women had the formal education necessary for the entrance. With the Campbell course, Croft hoped that more Bengali women would come forward to study medicine.

In 1893, Indulata Sen joined the Campbell Medical School on a scholarship of rupees seven a month plus school fees.

When he first heard about Indu's intentions of pursuing a course in medicine, Kartick was upset.

"Where is the need? You are almost twenty-four and it's time to start a family. Look at other women of your age, they all have children," he said to her.

"After what I have been through, I need a purpose in life to live. Also, we have to supplement our income. Social work with the Samaj hardly pays for two square meals a day. We need to earn more if we want to start a family. You have to support me in this venture." The second half of the argument carried weight with Kartick. He agreed.

Indu's class had fifteen new students and three old ones who had failed from the previous class. Women in Campbell studied the same subjects as their male counterparts including dissection. But they were excused from night duty.

In the first year class exams Indu stood third. In her second year, she was among the four students allowed to appear for the First Diploma Examination and she received the highest marks in both the papers—Anatomy & Physiology and Materia Medica.

During these years, Indu and Kartick lived in a Brahmo shelter, opened for Samaj workers. Along with her studies she also had to manage the housework. Her scholarship took care of some of the family expenses.

Tired after a day's work, she would often recount her classroom experiences to her husband—the fear and horror which she and her fellow students faced when examining a naked male corpse and how they had to overcome mental blocks of sex segregation and female modesty.

"We could manage only because William Sir was so gentle and patient with us," she told Kartick. William Andrews was one of the eminent British professors who taught at Campbell. He was especially fond of Indulata Sen. Apart from her interest and obvious intelligence, there was a certain sadness in her eyes which touched the professor.

Kartick did not take too kindly to the professor and made his dislike known to his wife. His response disillusioned her. She knew Kartick envied her success. Marriage had not been a rosy experience for her but she was determined to save it at all costs. "It is better to deal with one wolf than to be left at the mercy of a whole pack," she often consoled herself.

During her last year in college Indu found herself pregnant. Just before the results were declared, she gave birth to her first child, a son they named Keshub, after the Brahmo leader Keshub Chandra Sen.

Indulata Sen passed with flying colours and also the Viceroy's Silver Medal. She received permission to attend lectures at the Medical College.

But when it came to finding employment, it was a different story. Inspite of her academic brilliance, she had difficulty finding a job, disadvantaged mainly by race and gender. British and European male doctors were most in demand followed by Indian male doctors. Despite the rhetoric about the importance of female medical practitioners to care for female patients, Indian women doctors were not in high demand in the cities and were forced to look for jobs in the mofussil.

February 1907

The past two years have been spent mainly in illnesses. I have become severely anaemic due to erratic food habits and over exhaustion, leading to malnourishment. Though I am strict with my patients about their diets, I'm not able to follow it myself. Last year I also suffered a chronic bout of cholera and another miscarriage. I am tired and want to retire but with Kartick's failing health (he has been suffering from diabetes for some years now) and no job, I have to work to put food on the table. Besides, we have an extended family now. Apart from my three children, I have also adopted an orphan girl Hemangini and have taken in a sixteen-year-old abandoned child-widow, Jharna. Jharna has a few months old baby, Nayan.

Kartick is as moody and at times violent. I disapprove of his temper and occasional beatings, but I don't make a hue and cry of it. Where is the time after work for such things? Besides, I leave most of the decisions to Kartick, good or bad; I accept it as I have no other choice. I did not want to marry Kartick but I agreed to the marriage. It is my destiny and I accept it.

Most Indian medical practitioners could not afford the western trained nurses, midwives and compounders to run their hospitals in the mofussil areas. They depended on the local *dais*, *kavirajes* and *hakims*, whom the British considered quacks. Indulata and her contemporaries, however, took their help and sometimes sought advice on traditional folk remedies.

Even after so many years, Indulata's salary remained rupees eighty. Her health was rapidly degenerating and she was finding it increasingly difficult to cope with her job as well as her private practice. She sent Jharna to train as a nurse and one day told her, "You will have to accompany me on my private rounds since I cannot manage alone these days. That way you can learn too. After all you will have to hold fort and keep the practice running till Kundan becomes a doctor. Till then I would like to leave my patients to you."

"Don't say such things Ma. You'll be all right and you will hand over your practice to Kundan. Yourself," Jharna said.

Indulata just smiled.

December 1910

I turned forty this year and became a widow for the second time in my life. Kartick passed away in March due to complications from diabetes. The last few months of his life were painful with his kidneys failing in the end. Ours was not the happiest of marriages but he had been my husband for eighteen years. He was fifty-two when he died.

In 1912, Dr Peter Rawley, a British medical officer and a civil surgeon, was transferred to the Dufferin Women's Hospital in Hooghly—an extremely brash, arrogant man with little regard for the natives.

One day, Indulata was examining a female Muslim patient in her inner chamber, when Rawley suddenly barged in. "I need to have a word with you, Dr. Sen."

Indulata was furious. "How dare you come in like this without permission? Can't you see I am examining a patient?"

"I don't care about your patient and I don't need your permission to meet you. I am the Supervisor of this hospital," Rawley thundered.

"I don't care who you are. Don't forget this is a women's hospital and no man has a right to barge in like this when a woman is being examined," Indulata retorted.

"Don't talk to me like this, you ignorant woman…"

There was a resounding crack. Indulata had slapped him with all her might.

Indulata was forced to resign after the incident. However, she never once expressed regret over her behaviour. On the contrary, she enjoyed recounting this incident over and over again to amused, sometimes shocked, listeners.

Her stint as a "lady doctor" in the hospital came to an end. She directed all her energies to her private practice.

May 1915

I am depending more and more on Jharna to assist me in my private practice. In a few years' time Kundan will take over and I am waiting for that day to come. I have a nagging feeling that I may not live to see it.

My health is gradually deteriorating. Apart from anaemia, I am always fatigued, though my workload has decreased lately. I do not get sound sleep. My appetite has decreased and my left breast pains often. I know it has nothing to do with my heart, but my breasts feel soft and hurt when I touch them.

Krishmakali is happily settled in Dacca with her husband. He runs a successful family business. They have a daughter, Kajol, who is the apple of my eye.

Kundan has passed his matriculation examinations with flying colours and has expressed his interest to study medicine. I am so proud of him. May God be with him.

Jharna has been a pillar of strength and support to me, especially the way she has been handling my practice during my absence (which is getting more frequent these days). Her son Nayan and my adopted daughter, Hemangini, are in school.

God bless them all.

This was the last entry in the diary of Indulata Debi or the "lady doctor" as she was known in Chinsurah. Soon after she lost her life to a disease, which we can only conjecture to have been breast cancer. Nothing is known of the medical treatment she received for she did not write about the illness at all.

Remembering Little Dee

TWENTY-EIGHT DEVOTEES AND FOUR COMMANDOS KILLED AS TERRORISTS ATTACK THE SWAMINARAYAN TEMPLE AT AKSHARDHAM IN GUJARAT. PM TELLS MODI NOT TO ALLOW RERUN OF POST-GODHRA RIOTS AND EXERCISE RESTRAINT.
It seemed straight out of a violent Hindi film: children watch grandparents and three-year-old brother being gunned down by terrorists.

The headlines screamed in the morning papers. "How terrible..." sighed Brij, as he took off his spectacles and put the newspaper on the table. "It is a nightmare reading the papers these days. Terrorist attacks. Riots. Murders. Full of violence. What a way to start the day," Brij turned to his wife. "Sometimes I wonder what is the use of working hard and building a fancy house. It takes seconds for communal riots to erupt and in minutes your life's earnings are reduced to ashes."

"I know," Dee nodded in agreement. "No place in the world is safe now. Not after 9/11. Every conceivable place, every human being, has become vulnerable. No one is safe anywhere. What has the world come to, targetting places of worship? Did you see the look on the woman's face, the one who lost her three-year-old son, on TV last night?"

"Yes," Brij nodded.

"My heart went out to her. Her son was our Aman's age. It could have been Aman," Dee closed her eyes. "I shudder to think what I would have done had I been in her place."

"I know," said Brij. "I suggest you don't send Aman to the ISKCON temple in the evenings, at least for a few days."

"I was thinking on the same lines. But Aman will miss his visits. How does one explain these things to a child? Just imagine, these days one has to think twice before even visiting a place of worship."

They sat in silence for a while. Brij looked out at the sky from the terrace. It was slightly overcast. It is going to be a pleasant day, he thought. It was time, however, to get on with the daily business. "What would you like to have?" Dee interrupted his thoughts. "Eggs and toast or *paratha-dahi*?"

"I'm not particularly hungry. A cup of tea will be fine. Maybe an *aloo paratha* with it?"

Dee smiled. She knew he couldn't resist his *parathas*, the typical Punjabi that he was. "And I'm sure Madam will have her usual—tea with rusks. Honestly, Deepa, don't you ever tire of it?"

Dee laughed. It had been a long time since he had called her by her full name.

Deepa. Long time since she had heard it. Ever since she had come to the city, some seven years ago, all her friends and colleagues had ended up calling her Dee, a shortened version of an already short name. Or was it to sound more hip. Whatever the reason, she liked it and it had stuck. Nowadays, even her brother called her Dee. And much as she enjoyed an occasional toast and egg, sunny side up, for breakfast, Dee preferred her rusks—those browned and crisply toasted biscuits—and tea. Even when she stayed in five-star hotels during official tours and conferences, Dee preferred it. While her colleagues feasted on the large buffet spread, Dee would quietly have her rusks (which she always carried with her during her travels) dunked in tea, in the privacy of her room.

Because for Dee, rusk and *garam chai* went a long way back. Almost thirty years back, to a little village near Dhenkanal in Orissa.

Little Deepa was barely five, but she remembered it all so clearly. Deepa and her brother Raju would sit out in the garden of the Big

House, the Mohapatras' house as the villagers called it, waiting for their mother Nirmala to finish her chores. Nirmala was the cleaning woman—sweeping and mopping the floors as well as washing the utensils. She and her sister Bimala pitched in every morning at the Mohapatras' house between nine and noon.

Deepa's father was a farm hand on a daily wage. They had no land of their own, so her father tilled other people's land. But then work did not come every day; rather, for the better part of the year, Nirakar Mondal hardly had any work. And while he did not drink away whatever he earned, Nirakar was a lazy man. If he tried hard enough he could have supported his family, but the man loved to laze around during the day, and catch up with his friends in the evenings. From time to time he would visit his in-laws with his family, seeing to it that the children dressed in their ragged best, in order to arouse their sympathy. That way, he always took back something home by way of cash or kind to sustain himself and his family for a few more days.

This also was no doubt meagre, as his wife's family was hardly what you could call rich. But at least the male members of her family did not shy away from work, including his father-in-law, Motihari. Though on the wrong side of sixty, Motihari left at the crack of dawn, even before his sons woke up, to till his land; he would only return after sunset. Motihari tried to explain to Nirakar the value of hard work but to no avail.

"Since the Almighty has given you healthy limbs, you should make full use of them. Who knows, when they might become useless?"

These words of wisdom made no sense to Nirakar.

"It is easy for you to say so, Baba, because you are blessed with good health. Look at me. I am so much weaker. I feel dizzy in the sun. I feel faint if I stay out too long..."

"It is all in the mind, son. Good health or bad. All in the mind."

Nirmala was embarrassed by these visits and felt humiliated every time she visited her parents. She knew that her parents and brothers and their wives, treated her and her family little better than beggars, with loads of pity. And pity she did not want from anybody. And unknowingly, this was one quality she passed on to her daughter. Not money or jewels but a regard for hard work and the dignity of labour.

Once, when for days together the family went without food, Nirmala decided to find work for herself. Soon thereafter she started working for the Mohapatras as a housemaid. Her parents were not too happy with her decision. However, Nirakar did not show any displeasure. In fact, he was happy his wife had found work, which meant he could take it easy for some more time.

The Mohapatras chose to pay Nirmala and her sister in kind rather than cash. They were given half a seer of rice every day, with some raw vegetables and pulses thrown in once in a while. On festivals, the sisters got new saris and a little money by way of bonus. But they did not mind. For Nirmala, the food filled the empty stomachs of her children.

While their mother and aunt worked, Deepa and Raju would play around the garden, always careful not to step on the flowers and plants or trespass into the house. Sometimes, they sat and watched the children of the house playing. They were only a little older than the children, *and yet a whole wide world separated their lives. What it was like to be born privileged, Deepa could never imagine, and hence she never envied them. Save their fancy toys, especially the kitchen set the older daughter played with. "I don't want it, but I would like to play with it at least once," she aired her feelings to her mother.*

"Sssh. Don't even think of it," Nirmala would admonish her.

After Nirmala and Bimala finished their work, they would come out with two large, dented aluminium tumblers, filled with piping hot sugary tea. Raju and Deepa would run to them and wait for the older women to settle down. Both the sisters would untie their saree pallus and fish out crisp rusks. Four rusks each. Raju and Deepa would grab two each from their mother and aunt and devour them hungrily after dipping them in hot tea. The first bite was divine and was like nectar to their hungry bellies. The entire morning's wait was worth it for the children just to bite into those rusks.

"Good evening Madam, can I help you?" the young, polished salesman asked Dee as she entered the car showroom.

"I'm Mrs Khanna, Mr Brijmohan's wife. I think my husband spoke to you about the new car?"

"Oh yes, of course, Mrs Khanna. Do take a seat. What can I get you? Tea? Coffee? Or a soft drink?" asked the salesman.

"Oh nothing really. Thank you."

"What about the young man?" the salesman asked, turning to little Aman. "A Coke or a chocolate?"

"I want a Thums Up. And also a Kit Kat," Aman immediately chirped.

"Aman!" Dee gently rebuked him. "Oh, don't take him seriously."

"Oh that's alright Mrs Khanna. Why don't you have a cup of tea while you go through the brochures?"

"Okay."

"Maruti, *ek chai* for Madam and a Thums Up for baba, please," the salesman called to the peon.

Aman craned his neck towards her as Dee flipped through the brochure. She and Brij had already decided on the brand and model of the new car. All that was left was the colour, and Brij had left it to Dee to make the decision. "I know your tastes are sober—whatever you decide is fine by me," he had told her.

Looking at the various shade cards, Dee shortlisted a silver grey and a metallic beige. Suddenly a tiny little finger pointed to a bright red Viva, "Mummy, I want this one."

"Aman. Please. Sit down quietly."

Flopping back on his chair, Aman said cheerily, "You will take the red car no, Mummy? I like red colour. I want red colour car."

"Will you keep quiet and let me choose, please darling?" Dee was exasperated.

"But you choose red colour. It is a nice colour. I like red," Aman was persistent.

"What is the harm in red?" a voice behind Dee said. She turned around. It was Brij.

"Oh. It is you. When did you come in?"

"Just now." And he moved swiftly to pick up Aman who said, "Daddy, daddy, I want red car. Nice car. I want red car."

"Yes my darling, you will have your red car," Brij assured his son soothingly.

"But *jaan*," Dee looked bewildered. "You surely cannot be serious?"

"It's okay, honey. He likes the colour. What is the harm in buying it if it will make him happy?"

"But *jaan*, you don't seriously expect me to drive in that bright red contraption to office?"

"Oh come on, darling. No big deal. It is a nice bright colour. Besides, everyone chooses silver grey and metallic gold these days. You will be unique."

"You bet I will. And a laughing stock too."

"*Arre*. Come on now. Be a sport. Aman will be happy. Let him have his way," Brij cajoled her.

"Brij, don't you think he is too young to have his way? At this rate you will be spoiling him rotten. Imagine, at his age we didn't know...forget it. I don't want to argue. Do what you like," Dee said abruptly.

Lowering his voice, Brij said, "Listen honey, let us not argue and create a scene here. Besides, our parents did not have the money to indulge us. But just because of that, I do not want to deprive my son. I work hard for my family. It is different now...try and understand, Dee."

Of course things were very different for Aman than they had been for her in her childhood. Times had changed and life in an upper middle-class metro was a far cry from the village where she had been raised.

Dee saw herself clearly in her favourite blue frock, as her mother called it, almost twenty-five years back. It reached all the way down to her knees and had puffed sleeves and a nice sash, which she could tie into a bow at the back. Sprinkled with tiny flowers in dark blue over a pale blue background, it had been given to her by the Mohapatra Ginnima during rathajatra or the festival of chariots of Lord Jagannatha. It had come from the big city of Cuttack and was meant for the older girl. But it had turned out to be too short for her and too long for her younger sister, so the lady of the house had given it to Nirmala to give to her daughter. Ginnima often saw Deepa and her brother playing in the garden, and though they tried to keep out of her way, she always had a few kind words and a smile for them. From time to time Ginnima would give some of the older daughter, Sabitri's dresses to Deepa, but the blue one remained her favourite for a long time.

When Deepa was ten, she started working in a small teashop just outside their village near the station. Raju, older to her by a year and a half, had already started working in the shop some six months earlier. During the day, he waited on the few customers who frequented the shop.

For this, he received two cups of tea with a few biscuits during the day and a lunch comprising a bowl of rice and dal, an onion and a couple of raw green chillies. He also received five rupees a month, which made him the highest earning member in the family.

Gopalbabu, the owner, not only made him serve tea but also do the dishes and keep the place clean. He had to sweep and swab the shop twice daily. When there were no customers, Gopalbabu would yell, "Oye chokra. Why are you sitting idle? Don't you know an idle mind is a devil's workshop. Go. Go and help your boudi at the back." Boudi *meaning his wife and back meaning the two little rooms which made up Gopalbabu's living quarters, just behind the teashop. Boudi's work was never ending and her complaints perennial. Raju would help the woman with many of her household chores. He washed the dishes, cubed the vegetables, stirred food cooking on the kerosene stove, while* boudi *breast-fed her new-born baby.*

If a customer dropped in unexpectedly, Gopalbabu would hit the roof. "Arre, O Raju, where are you, you rascal? Again you've gone out to play?" Raju would then have to drop whatever he was doing mid-way and run to attend to the customer. As he ran, boudi's *voice would follow him. "Orre muhkpora, (burnt-faced one) why do you leave midway. Can't you complete the job?"*

Deepa missed her brother deeply, especially while she waited for her mother at the Mohapatras'. One day, while dropping Raju at the teashop, they heard the owner's wife cribbing about the load of housework and that she could do with some help. Deepa quickly volunteered, much against her mother's wishes. "Girls from our family don't work," Nirmala admonished her.

"But I get so bored without Raju. Atleast this way I will be engaged and will also be earning something," she pleaded. The thought of contributing towards the family financially was embedded early on in their minds, a thought born out of deprivation and necessity.

Thus Deepa started earning from the time she was ten. Nirakar managed to work out the same deal for Deepa with Gopalababu as for Raju, and at the end of each month happily pocketed their earnings. The children did not mind, but once in a way they too longed to buy something for themselves.

For sometime now, Deepa and Raju had been eyeing a red motorcar, which ran after being wound up with a key. Just like the one Sabitri's brother, Chotokarta, the small lord, had. Chotokarta had bought it from the annual mela held in the next village during the rathajatra.

That year the mela was on and the children longed to visit the fair. For the first time, both brother and sister plucked up enough courage to ask Gopalababu for their salary. "Why? Why should I hand it over to you children? Let your father come and collect it."

"No, Gopalbabu, Baba is busy. He told us to tell you to give the money to us. He needs it," Deepa said trying to maintain a brave front.

Gopalbabu muttered something under his breath as he reluctantly handed over the ten rupees.

"Chal. Let's go," Deepa motioned to Raju and they scampered off to the fair.

"I don't think it is right, what we are doing. We should go home and give the money to Baba, otherwise he will get angry," Raju said innocently.

"Arre bhai, do not worry. We are not going to spend all of it. Just a bit. After all, it is our money. We earn it. We can enjoy it once in a while. Let's go to the mela," Deepa reassured her brother. Raju shrugged and followed. At that early age too, the trend was set for a lifetime—Deepa would always lead and Raju would follow. Later, Raju would have a lot of catching up to do.

What followed that afternoon was what every child's dream is made of. They enjoyed themselves immensely as they rode the giant wheel, admired the wares at the stalls and ate paapri chaat till they were ready to burst. All this in just fifty paise and there were still nine rupees, fifty paise left. "I think we should return home now. Otherwise our folks will start to worry," Raju told his sister.

"Just one moment," Deepa said and scampered off to one of the toy shops. After a few minutes she returned very excited with her loot. "See what I bought?" she said holding up the bright red car for her brother. "Now we too will have our own car which will run once it is wound up with this key here. Just like Chotokarta's." Unable to contain her excitement, she wound it up to show her brother. Both children then took turns playing with their new toy.

"How much did it cost? Must be expensive?" Raju asked.

"Yes, a bit. One rupee fifty paise. But only this once. I always wanted a chabiwala car," Deepa explained.

"Alright. It is getting late. We can play with it once we reach home," Raju told Deepa as they headed towards their village.

However, they were not prepared for what was in store for them. Nirakar flew into a rage when he learnt that they had gone to the fair by themselves, and even more so, because they had spent money on their own. "At your age, we never knew what money was, leave alone handling it," he screamed. Even Nirmala spoke up.

"You know how difficult our days are. We cannot put food in our mouths and you go and buy fancy toys," she admonished.

"Go right now and return that car to the shop and get back that rupee and a half. One whole rupee and fifty paise! How can you spend all that money on a silly car? Go at once before it gets too dark," Nirakar was hysterical.

Deepa was in tears. "Please, let me keep it just this once. I promise I will not buy any more toys. I have always wanted this. Please Baba, please. You know I do not have any toys apart from that headless doll."

"Nothing doing You keep that car and we will go hungry for days. Go right now and return it," Nirakar was adamant.

"I told you not to buy it," Raju tried his best to console his sister, as they headed towards the fair again. Several times on the way, Deepa rubbed the car's wheels against her favourite blue frock to remove any tell-tale signs of grime. But when they reached the toy stall, they found to their great dismay that the shopkeeper refused to take the car back or return the money. "Goods once sold cannot be returned or exchanged," he said point blank.

"Please," Raju begged. "Our parents will be very angry. We will not be able to go back home if we do not take back the money with us. Please sir, try to understand."

This was too much for little Deepa. She started crying piteously. A crowd began to gather near the toyshop. While Raju tried explaining to the crowd and Deepa howled incoherently, the shopkeeper felt embarrassed. Fearing he may lose out on prospective customers, he *quickly handed over a rupee and a half to the girl and snatched the car. "Never show your face again," he thundered. Deepa quickly wiped her tears and holding hands, the two children started running towards their village. Halfway through, Deepa suddenly broke the silence, "At least I could play with it for some time."*

The brother and sister smiled at each other.

"I said write A, not V. *Kitne bar samjhao tumhe?*" said Dee, irritated. Unaffected, Aman wrote yet another shaky V with his stubby little fingers and total concentration.

"*Arre* baba, Aman this is V, not A. You are writing it *ulta*, upside down. *Chalo*. Write it properly. Like this," and she held his hand and traced an A on the book.

"A," Aman said gleefully.

"Yes," Dee smiled. "Now write B like I taught you." With full confidence Aman traced a mirror image of the alphabet B. Smiling, he showed it to his mother.

"Oh dear! Upside down again. You know your alphabets. Then why do you get them upside down? C'mon, try again. See, like this." Aman responded with another upside down B.

Dee was exasperated, "It's such a simple thing. Why can't you get it right? Bad boy. Bad Aman."

"I am not bad," Aman tried to defend himself.

"Yes, you are. Mamma cannot teach you anymore," Dee said, turning her back on her son.

Tears trickled down the little boy's face. "No, you will

teach me Mamma. Please. I am not bad." He tried to put his chubby arms around her.

"Yes, you are," Dee said, irritated, shrugging his arms off. Aman burst into fresh tears. Suddenly Dee turned around and picked up her son. "Sorry beta. I didn't mean to. I am so sorry," and she patted and kissed the boy, "Shh, shh. Don't cry. Mamma is sorry. Aman is not a bad boy at all. Aman is Mamma's clever little baby, isn't he?"

Aman nodded through sobs.

What's the matter with me, Dee thought, quite alarmed with what she had just done. It is not like me to shout at my son. What is happening to me? I used be the epitome of patience. I used to give four tuitions a day as a teenager after school to pay for my studies. And now with all the help in the house, I cannot even have five minutes of patience with my son. Something is wrong with me. Complacency, I suppose.

One day, a few months after Deepa started working in the tea shop, Ginnima enquired about the children, especially Deepa. "Why don't you bring the children along anymore Nirmala? I hope all is well?" Nirmala told Ginnima about their employment. "Chhee, chhee, Nirmala. How can you let your young daughter work? Soon she will be of marriageable age. What will people say?" When Nirmala explained her predicament, Ginnima came up with a solution. Deepa would be sent to her older sister's house in Cuttack as domestic help. "That way she will live comfortably and help Didi with the housework.

They are quite well-off and they will treat her like a family member. When you find a boy for her, she can come back to marry. Till then, let her learn some housework."

Nirakar did not like the idea of their daughter going away to a big city. But Nirmala persisted. "She will be better off in a house rather than at Gopalbabu's shop, for all the men to ogle at."

Thus began Dee's dream-like journey, from her village to the city, from penury to wealth. But that would take a long time. All Dee had were fond memories of Cuttack, of Boro Ginnima, as she called Ginnima's elder sister.

Boro Ginnima was a kind lady. Since both her children were grown and studying in Calcutta, Boro Ginnima treated Deepa like a daughter. She was the old lady's personal maid, massaging her feet, oiling and plaiting her thinning mane, ironing her sarees and sometimes accompanying her to the cinema or the market. It was at Boro Ginnima's insistence that Deepa was put in a local school, where among other subjects she also learnt English, which turned out to be her favourite subject. Boro Ginnima's daughter, Dolly, was doing her Master's in English Literature at the university in Calcutta. When Dollydidi came home during the holidays and spoke fluent English just like those TV newsreaders, Deepa resolved that one day she too would read, write and speak in English like her. Then she would get herself a good job with a high salary. To her, English was the passport to success and wealth.

Boro Ginnima was happy with Deepa's academic progress. She was intelligent and sincere. Though a late starter, she was given double promotions quite a few times and matriculated with honours. At eighteen, she was older than most girls in her class who were preparing for marriage and motherhood. Nirakar insisted she return home. He had found a boy for her. The marriage date would be fixed soon.

The thought of marriage terrified Deepa. How could she spend the rest of her life with an illiterate villager, having tasted city life and education? But even Boro Ginnima would not listen to her. "Enough is enough. Now do as your parents say. After all, I cannot oppose them. You are their daughter." Besides, Boro Ginnima was too busy preparing for her elder son, Santosh's wedding. The bride had been chosen, the wedding date had been fixed and shopping for the trousseau was in full swing. No one had time for Deepa.

One lazy summer afternoon, when the household was asleep, Deepa packed her meagre belongings in a small bag, along with some money she had saved over the years, and quietly slipped away from Boro Ginnima's life. She took the bus to Bhuvaneswar and then a train to Calcutta. She had Dollydidi's Calcutta address and contact number and soon found her way to Dollydidi's Ladies' Hostel.

When Dolly saw her, she was shocked out of her wits. "Deepa! You? What on earth are you doing here?" After hearing her story, she tried to persuade her to return home. But Deepa was adamant. Finally Dolly relented and agreed to help her with further studies.

"But you will have to earn your living and pay for your education. I can only set you up initially," Dolly told her. "I will do anything to get away from my miserable life. Just guide me, Didi."

Deepa began life in the metro as a part-time housemaid. Dolly managed to get her admitted into a government college where the tuition fee was heavily subsidised. She did her intermediate in arts, planning to major in English Literature, failing which she would opt for History.

Life was hard. Deepa rose at the crack of dawn and went to the Ghoshs' house to do their cleaning. Then she ran a few errands for the Dattas next door. She would come back to the hostel to help Bulumashi, the old maid, with the cleaning, in lieu of which she was given free accommodation, sharing a dormitory bed and a bath with twelve other girls.

After a frugal breakfast in the common mess, Deepa would leave for college around nine, not returning before four in the afternoon. A few months into college and she had taken up four private tuitions, which took care of her college fees, as well as her survival in the city. She enjoyed teaching junior students and was so friendly and patient that she soon became a favourite with them. She seldom returned before nine in the evening, almost always so tired that she would fall asleep the moment her head touched the pillow. Since she could not afford the dinner at the hostel mess, very often she went without dinner. In fact, one of the reasons she looked forward to her tuitions was the food that accompanied tea at her students' houses.

"Lovely weather, isn't it *jaan*?" Brij suddenly turned to Dee, as they drove down the clear Goa-Mumbai road. "We will have a pleasant stay in Chiplun. The lake will look lovely at this time of the day. I'm sure we'll be in time to see the sun set."

"Hmm," Dee nodded.

"I like the hotel there. It is so quaint and comfortable. And the best part is the bed. So huge and so comfortable, just right to loll about. I hate small hotel beds. You cannot even turn comfortably. Did you notice the one in our Goa hotel? Really cramped."

"Hmm," returned Dee.

"Hey, what is the matter?" Brij reached for Dee's hand in the back seat of their luxurious Safari. "Are you alright?"

"Oh yes. Absolutely. Nothing is the matter. In fact I was just admiring the view."

"Ah. My contemplative wife," Brij mocked, gently.

"I hope you enjoyed yourself at Goa. Especially the New Year's eve night. Some *tamasha* it was, but fun nevertheless. Don't you think so?" Brij asked Dee after a while.

"Of course I did," Dee answered.

"I had always wanted to drive down to Goa, especially after I bought this Safari. Ravi and Sabishi have done it so often, and so have Neeraj and Chitra. Neeraj always prefers to drive to Goa than take the train. It is a lovely drive. Don't you think so?" Brij asked.

"Yes. But rather long, isn't it?" Dee replied.

"Yes. But I guess that is the fun of it."

"It does get a bit tiring at the end. I'd rather fly down or take the train next time."

"Really Dee! You amaze me. How can you find such a beautiful drive tiring? In any case, we do not need to do more than six hours of driving a day. Both ways we halted at Chiplun and we did not drive at a stretch for more than two hours. How do you mean tiring?"

"I know...but we are not getting any younger," Dee shrugged.

"What do you mean, not getting younger? Look at the roads. Smooth. No bumps. It is a dream driving on this stretch. Besides, look at this car. It is such a luxurious car, just meant for long drives. Comfortable seats, lots of leg room, great cooling system and a VCD to watch films. What more can you ask for? Look how much Aman is enjoying himself."

"I know and I see your point Brij. But... well..."

"Well what?"

"Well, life has got a bit too comfortable these past few years. Flying around the place in business class. Even short distances like Pune, which I would cover by car or the Deccan Queen earlier, is now just a flight away. I know I sound obnoxious, but I have lost my sense of adventure; or the ability to compromise even for small things. To think of all the hardships I have been through to get here. It amazes me to think that fifteen years ago I used to cycle forty kilometres every Sunday with the sun blazing overhead and look now...the most comfortable chauffeur-driven air-conditioned vehicle. Yet, I am tired. Brij, I am getting scared. I am losing a very important part of myself. My tolerance level. I am growing indifferent to life."

"I understand honey," Brij comforted her as he reached for her hand.

"Do you? Do you really Brij? Because I don't think I do myself."

After she had completed her graduation, Dolly asked Deepa if she had given a serious thought to her career. "No. I really haven't thought about it. Maybe I will do my MA."

"It is all very well to say 'I'll do my MA'. But where will you get the funds from? Scholarships are rare in English Literature. Besides, after doing your MA you will be limited to academics. Only girls from affluent families waiting to get married can think of doing their MA. You need to do a professional course which will help you get a good job. This city is not like your village. Here money rules and if you want to survive here you have to join the rat race. Bujli?"

Deepa nodded. It was Dollydidi again who insisted on her doing a course at a management institute. "MBA is now the latest fad—it is the new path to golden opportunities." She told her about the weekly year-long course in management conducted under the aegis of a well known management institute abroad. "Only, it is far out. Beyond Baranagar. Every Sundays between 10 AM to 6 PM. At the end of the year they will give you a diploma which will open up many doors for your career. Besides, the faculty comprises the best brains from the field, some even from the IIMs. That is why they are available only on Sundays.

"Also a lot of companies sponsor their employees. If you join the course, you will learn of many such opportunities. But getting you in

this course is not going to be easy," Dolly said. After a lot of effort, Dolly was able to persuade some of her influential friends to give letters of recommendation to her ward. "She is a very bright and hardworking girl, but poor. This is a once in a lifetime opportunity for her," she explained.

"I can never thank you enough Dollydidi. I will always remain indebted to you," Deepa said.

"So long as you utilise it fully, I will be happy. And no question of being indebted. The only way you can repay me is by helping someone else in need when you are in a position to help."

"I will remember that," said Deepa.

"How will you go there? It is quite far. Nearly forty kilometres. You will have to change buses atleast three times and it can become quite expensive. There is no direct train there. You will end up wasting a lot of time in travel...let us see."

"Why can't I borrow your cycle for the day. I cycle well," Deepa added.

"Are you mad! On that bicycle? Do you know how long it will take you? Hours. And in this heat? You will be so tired. How will you concentrate on the lectures?" Dolly asked, surprised.

"Dollydidi, don't worry. Leave it to me. I will leave early, and besides I cycle quite well. It will be good exercise. Would you lend me the cycle on Sundays, please?"

"That is okay by me. But do you think cycling alone all that distance will be safe, especially for a young woman?" Dollydidi asked, concerned.

"Nothing can be worse than having to return to my village. And after coming this far...No didi, don't discourage me. I have to make something of my life. I have seen my mother suffer. I do not want a life like her's."

Deepa rose a little late on weekdays now that her college was over. But she still continued with her private tuitions, in fact they had trebled by now as her reputation as a competent and patient tutor spread. She would leave around ten in the mornings and not return before ten at night. She had, however, stopped working as a housemaid, though she still helped with cleaning in the hostel. This was more for self-discipline than anything else. With her earnings from her tuitions she was comfortable and was looking at sharing a room like Dollydidi rather than a common dormitory.

Her Sundays were busy too. Waking up early, she would shower, help in cleaning the hostel and have a light breakfast. Packing a lunch of about half a dozen soft, thick rotis and mango pickle, she would set off on her cycle, the dupatta shielding her face from the sun. After nearly two hours of non-stop and brisk cycling, she would reach the outskirts of Baranagar.

When some of her fellow students learnt about it they wondered how she managed. Wasn't it tiring, they asked. She would laugh it off. It was fun, she said.

Now even she wondered, how did she do it then? Was it the same Deepa? Or maybe it was plain Deepa Mondal of yore, so unlike Mrs Dee Khanna of today. Dee smiled to herself at the thought.

Brij was watching her affectionately. "A penny for your thoughts," he said.

"Life's been one helluva journey for me."

Radha's Journey

It was one of those hot June afternoons in Delhi. The moment you step out into the open, a hot breeze, locally called "loo", slaps your face. By eleven in the morning the streets are deserted. The only people who venture out do so not because they want to, but because they have no alternative. And even then they do not waste their time sauntering but take brisk strides to their destinations, with moist scarves wrapped around their heads. Yes, we are talking of times when the mercury can soar up to anywhere between forty to forty-five degree Celsius at any given time of the day. When coolers and airconditioners sometimes pack up due to the excess heat. When the heat can even strike people dead.

It was on one such afternoon that Radha Pal lay lazily stretched on the divan, her long limbs relaxing, her kohl-rimmed eyes staring absentmindedly at the ceiling fan whirring. She remembered her childhood when she and her younger sister would brave the scorching heat and venture out to play. While the elders complained about the heat, Radha and Rina were so engrossed in their games that they did not even feel it.

Not any longer though. Radha had passed her childhood years, crossed her moody teens, overcome her difficult twenties. Now somewhere in her mid-thirties, life had taken quite a turn. The years had mellowed her steely self and she could no longer tolerate the Delhi summers. Having spent the last couple of summers mostly in the air-conditioned comforts of five-star hotels in Bombay and other cities, she had got thoroughly spoilt. A feeling she revelled in, though she tried to give the impression of not being interested in material comforts—in keeping with the socialist leanings she professed for herself.

Radha was beginning to look at life from an altogether new perspective. Just like the house she was in at the moment. It was new along with its furniture and accessories. A part of a new set of apartment blocks, away from downtown Delhi. The whole block including her home smelt of fresh paint, like the newly acquired riches of its inhabitants. They were mostly what one would call the nouveau riche, having suddenly come into wealth. These people had earlier either lived in the less affluent areas of Delhi in dilapidated tenements or migrated from villages nearby to make it big in the city.

She had bought this apartment about six months back, from her earnings from the past couple of years as a dance choreographer in the Bombay film industry. It was a spacious 2BHK apartment, with two bedrooms, a living room or, as urban Indians preferred to call it, a hall and a kitchen.

It was airy and well-lit and since this was a developing area, there were no buildings nearby. It's a great relief not to look into your neighbour's kitchen or bedroom the moment you opened your window, thought Radha.

Since she had dipped into most of her savings and there was no other immediate source of income—she had taken a breather from films for a while and it was a lean time on the relationships front too—she decided to keep the major restructuring work for a later date. Instead she had done up her house with affordable, brightly coloured handloom cushions and curtains, *dhurries* and simple cane furniture, for a chic, yet elegant look. Her one big indulgence, however, was a two-ton air-conditioner, which she installed in her bedroom and she seldom ventured out of this room during the summer afternoons.

Radha put her feet up on the cane divan and fiddled with the TV remote, aimlessly surfing channels. While the dipping temperature in the room was gradually numbing her body, her mind felt alert and active. Carelessly, she gathered her long black tresses and knotted them around the nape of her neck. As she did so her eyes fell on the photo album lying on the nearby table.

She had taken it out from her bag while she was unpacking. Radha had just returned from a fortnight's shooting schedule in Bombay. Wherever she went, the album travelled with her, locked up in her suitcase, away from people's gazes. Its contents too had been stored away in the darkest recesses of her memory. She had been so busy with work that nothing but the present mattered to her.

She casually flicked through it. There she was at six years with her parents and Rina, still a toddler, in their mother's arms; with long braids folded up in pigtails with bright blue ribbons in school uniform, the darkest among the other girls with a glistening white toothy smile; as an awkward teenager with her friend Sneha, trying to look hip but distinctly uncomfortable in a pair of peddle-pushers and baggy white top.

Her eyes then fell on the photograph where she wore a bright red silk sari with a simple gold border, flowers in her hair and a garland around her neck. The man next to her wore a white kurta-pyjama, a garland around his neck too. By her side was her best friend Sneha, Sneha's boyfriend Kushal and their common friend, Anwar. "Where have all these people gone?" thought Radha to herself. "I am not in touch with them now. Yet there was a time when I couldn't imagine the world without them. They were my friends. My soulmates. And Aloke," she sighed as she looked carefully at the man with the garland next to her, "He was my best friend."

Her earliest memories of her parents were those of incessant bickering. She must have been three or four then. Parvati, Radha's mother, was a woman with a strong mind of her own, a trait her daughter inherited. She wouldn't take any nonsense from anyone, and that included her husband.

Parvati Menon was a dark, lissome Keralite who had been brought up in Bombay. Her father had come to the city from Cochin as a young lad, joined Union Carbide as a trainee and, after forty years of service, retired from the same company as a senior executive. He was not rich by Bombay standards, but the family had a comfortable middle-class existence. Parvati and her sisters attended a local English-medium school and Parvati had plans to study comparative literature. Her parents wanted their eldest to marry a Menon boy of their choice. Never having disobeyed her parents before, this was one occasion where Parvati decided to put her foot down.

While studying at the university, she had got friendly with a fellow student from Calcutta, Sunil Pal. Sunil was dark, short and stout, with an unruly mop of hair, a shaggy beard and wild eyes. He was not polished like her other friends and could hardly speak English. He came from a small village and his innate intelligence and way with words had fetched him a government scholarship to the university.

He lacked in social graces, was unrefined in his ways—yet there was an underlying sexual energy in him which women found exciting. Parvati happened to be one of them. Sunil on his part found her middle-class sobriety a refreshing change.

When Parvati declared her love for Sunil to her parents, they first tried to wean her away from him by gentle persuasion. When they realised the futility of it, they simply refused to entertain him. Not to be outdone, Parvati decided to elope with her beau. Initially, Sunil also tried dissuading her as he did not have a steady job. But Parvati was adamant. So they quietly got married and Parvati moved out of her Colaba home into a small Dongri *chawl* with Sunil.

Life was hard for the couple, having to live in a one-room tenement and share a bath with five other families. The surroundings were squalid and provided no privacy to a newly married couple. Sunil survived on odd jobs like freelance copywriting and pamphlet-writing, dreaming of being a famous poet someday. He had expected some monetary gains out of his alliance with Parvati. When nothing came of it and his initial sexual urges were satiated, he decided to look elsewhere for his "creative inspiration". Frequent quarrels started.

Within these circumstances Radhika Pal—Radha—was born. Almost a year after her birth, the Menons somewhat reconciled towards Parvati and, in the guise of meeting their granddaughter, invited Parvati and Radha to their Colaba rentals on afternoons when Sunil was away. The Menons still refused to accept their son-in-law, whose antecedents were unclear and whom they considered a good-for-nothing.

When Radha was two, Sunil Pal was offered a job with an advertising agency in Delhi as a copywriter. Though he did not consider the job worthy of his talents, he nevertheless decided to accept it for want of anything better.

Life was not easy for the Pals in Delhi, though it was a tad better than what it had been in Bombay. Relations between Sunil and Parvati grew more strained. When Radhika was five, her sister Rina was born. Maybe a second child would soften Sunil, thought Parvati, though she knew he desired a son. But Sunil's erratic behaviour continued. He blamed his wild ways on his creative urges and took out his frustrations on his wife and family.

Asha Grewal was a socialite, twice divorced and a suspect in the murder case of her last husband. She had reportedly caught him in bed with another woman. Delhi society could not stop talking about this event for months together. This incident, ironically, seemed to improve her visibility in the media—she became a Page 3 celebrity.

Sunil and Asha were frequently seen together at parties, arm-in-arm with each other. She, an impeccably dressed, hard-faced beauty. He, wild, errant dilettante. They made an odd but distinct pair. After a few drinks, Sunil would invariably turn his attention to any woman he came across. However, he always made up to Asha afterwards. She was his golden goose, his stepping stone to a good life and wealth, things which Parvati could not give him. A life he yearned for and was willing to grab at the cost of his family. For Sunil was a ruthless man as far as emotions were concerned. A legacy he unwittingly passed on to his daughter.

When Radha was ten, Parvati decided to move out with the children. Sunil did not object, as by then he was moving on in life too. The children supported their mother wholeheartedly. At that tender age they were wise enough to feel her pain. They refused to have anything to do with their father, including his name. They preferred to be called Menon.

For the third time in her life Parvati had to set up house afresh. She found employment in an NGO and managed to support herself and her children. During school holidays, she sent them to her parents' place in Bombay, though she seldom accompanied them. She avoided her parents as she could not stand their we-told-you-so looks. Life, though hard, moved smoothly, while Sunil climbed the social and financial ladder with amazing speed. But the developments in his life had taken a toll on his health and Asha was not doing much to soothe his nerves. The result was diabetes with high blood sugar levels.

A few months later, Sunil quit his job to write poetry full time and, at Asha's insistence, moved in with her. In their circle of friends, he came to be jocularly referred to as "the resident poet". With Asha's social contacts, he managed to land some lucrative book assignments from well-known publishers. She also arranged for his poetry readings at exclusive dos of top industrial houses. His works were commissioned by prestigious publications. This inspite of the fact that by now the quality of his work had deteriorated considerably. His poetic brilliance had dulled as he spent most of his waking hours drinking and womanising. It did not matter to his readers, that section of society which went by the hype and hoopla surrounding an author's works rather than the merit of his books.

Sunil's example proved to be a lesson in life for Radha. She learnt early to get what she wanted at whatever cost. A lesson that would stand her in good stead in future.

School was a routine and uneventful affair and Radha was an average student. But by the time she reached college, the ugly duckling became a swan—tall, slim and pretty. The buck teeth settled in, her features grew more defined. Her *kohl*-lined doe-eyes, pert little nose, crooked smile and waist-length silky hair added to her beauty. Ethnic jewellery and clothes complimented her dusky complexion. Radha knew she could turn heads and set many a heart aflutter almost effortlessly.

Boys were at her beck and call all the time and she revelled in the attention. They bought her coffee or lunch, took her to the movies, drove her around on their bikes and lent her notes. At times Parvati worried when she saw so many men hovering around her pretty daughter, but Radha assured her mother that she was old enough to handle them herself.

After her graduation, Radha decided to do a teachers' training course for want of anything better. Around this time, she started taking part in college plays and student rallies. It was during the rehearsals for one such play that she met Aloke Jha, a Maithil Brahmin from Bihar. Aloke was tall and wiry with gentle features. He hailed from a modest family from Purnea and was pursuing a Masters' course in Economics in Delhi University. Aloke was popular with the students and was president of a local student's body. Like many others, Aloke too was smitten by Radha's charms.

One thing led to another and they both decided to get married. Parvati would hear none of it. She felt that her daughter deserved far more than a left-wing youth leader with impractical ideals and an empty wallet. She asked

Sunil to intervene, but he was indifferent. Aloke's parents also did not want a highly educated city-bred girl as their *bahu*. They preferred that he marry a simple girl from their community who would be adept at household chores. Besides, Radha belonged to a different caste.

But love was young—and heady. And the heart prevailed over the mind. The young lovers tied the knot in a simple ceremony, exchanging garlands at the local marriage registry office. The witnesses were Radha's best friend, Sneha, her boyfriend, Kushal and Aloke's best man, Anwar. No rings were exchanged or *mangalsutra* tied as Aloke did not believe in such customs. The feast was a simple lunch at Dwarka outside the campus. The honeymoon was in Aloke's PG digs, a modest one-room affair near Vasant Kunj. Thus began another chapter in the life of Radhika Pal, now Jha.

Aloke's landlady, Mrs Gulati, housed her paying guests in the small room (normally meant for the domestic staff) that lay outside her spacious three-bedroomed apartment. Earlier this room with a separate entrance was used for her outstation guests. Ever since her daughter had got married and moved to the US, she had converted her daughter's room to a guest room. Her son was in college and since she had enough time on her hands, she did not mind the occasional relative who turned up. To supplement her pocket-money, she used the outside room for paying guests. The extra Rs 1,000 that came in each month kept Mrs Gulati happy, and she promptly invested the sum by joining another kitty group. The PGs were also happy with their tiny private haven.

Mrs Gulati had one stipulation though. The room was to be rented to single persons, preferably males. She became quite fond of Aloke as he mostly kept to himself and never bothered her. However, when his bride moved in with him, she protested mildly. "This was not part of our agreement, beta."

"I know Aunty. Just give me a little time and we will shift soon. This is a little small for us."

"Alright. But look for a place soon."

After six months Aloke had still not found a place for himself and Radha. The reason being that he had not found a job yet to be able to afford the rent. Very few jobs agreed with the temperament of this young idealist. In interviews, his strong views would scare prospective employers. Besides, a certain complacency had set in and he preferred to hang out with his theatre activist friends rather than hunt for a job.

The first flush of love over, Radha was getting a little impatient with Aloke. She had nothing to do at home but sit and read. She stopped attending her TTC course midway. Since they were not allowed to cook in the room apart from making tea or coffee, she had no housework. Besides, she dreaded the funny looks Mrs Gulati gave her every time she left the house and the snide remarks that followed. "Look, look. Madam turns up in new sarees everyday with *gajra* in her hair even when they can't afford a bigger place to live in."

Of late, Radha had taken to wearing sarees as Aloke insisted on it. Though tying it was difficult initially, she had mastered the art of casually draping it over herself, to her best advantage. She loved the appreciative glances that she received, especially from smart and rich young men.

Hari Menon, a young and upwardly mobile business executive from Wharton, was one such man. Radha loved his dark good looks, his wit and humour. Sanjay Narula, scion of one of Delhi's wealthiest families, was another of her admirers. She forgave his goofiness because she appreciated his ability to spend money on her. Robin Nanda, with his sexy looks and impeccable dress sense, was yet another. She overlooked the little incident when one night, in a drunken stupor, Robin had driven his spanking new BMW over a couple of street urchins. Though the urchins did not survive, he was acquitted because of his influential connections.

Both Sanjay and Robin were engaged to be married shortly, but they enjoyed her company. The fact that she was married suited them even better as it meant they could carry on a liaison with no strings attached. Hari was of a more serious temperament. But he had just broken off with his girlfriend of several years and did not want to commit himself in a hurry. He discovered, quite accidentally, that Radha was married and was not amused by the fact that she had kept it under wraps.

Radha was intelligent enough to understand that most of these men were looking to have a fling with her. These relationships promised nothing more. Also, she was a perfect combination of beauty and brains. Barring Hari, these young men were a shallow lot and were in awe of her as much for her exotic looks as her cultivated highbrow talk.

The moolah started coming in and Radha could buy herself the most expensive clothes. She started developing expensive habits. Mrs Gulati noticed gleaming chauffeur-driven cars come to pick up Radha in the afternoons, mostly when Aloke was away. Tongues wagged. Aloke was first suspicious, then jealous, and finally hurt when Radha refused to share any information about her friends. The couple fought and the fights refused to get resolved. Radha realised that she had married in haste. She had believed in his intellect and ideals and had hoped that he would do something worthwhile in life. But nothing seemed to be happening and she wanted to move on.

"I think we need to give ourselves some space. We need to think things over," Radha told Aloke one morning.

"Are you saying you are tired of me? Already?" he asked.

"I am not saying any such thing. All I am saying is that we need some space. I need to think things over myself..."

"Do what you like," and with that he slammed the door and walked out.

Radha packed whatever little she had in a suitcase, hailed a cab and headed for Sneha's place. Mrs Gulati watched her leave with glee.

Sneha tried to talk Radha into patching up with Aloke. "These little arguments happen in all marriages," she counselled. "I suggest you go back home."

"No way. I need a little time to myself. All along I've been someone's daughter, someone's wife. Let me be myself for a while now," she said, rather expansively. She also realised that she could not stay with Sneha for too long. So a few days later, she mustered up courage and rang Parvati at work.

"Amma..." she choked over the phone.

"What's the matter, child?" Parvati asked and listened with alarm to the sound of her daughter's stifled sobs.

Later that evening Radha entered her mother's modest apartment, overwhelmed with tears. Parvati gave her time to get over her anger and hurt and one day asked her, "When are you returning to Aloke?"

"I am not going back to him."

"But why?"

"Because he doesn't care about me. He doesn't bother to look for a job. All he does is spend time with those loafers in that theatre group," Radha complained.

"But he's young. Give him some time. You shouldn't have got married in such a hurry."

"I realise that now."

"Then go back and explain your problems to him. You must learn to adjust. Marriage is all about adjusting," Parvati tried to reason with her daughter.

"Please amma. I'm not going back. If you don't want me here, I'll live elsewhere. But I'm not going back to Aloke."

"I don't understand you kids at all. You are all in such a hurry. No patience. No tolerance. I tried adjusting with your father's whims for ten years before I opted out and you won't even give your marriage a year?" But she knew better than to push her daughter any further. She heard Radha mumble, "Just give me a little time. I'll find a job. Once I start earning, I'll move out."

Parvati enjoyed her job with the NGO and worked long hours. Radha would go out with her friends in the evenings and not be home till the wee hours. Most days mother and daughter hardly met as Radha would be sleeping when

Parvati left for work and Parvati would be in bed by the time Radha returned.

A few days went by. Parvati noticed certain changes in her daughter. She mostly wore revealing outfits, had permed her hair and wore loud make-up. Things unaccounted for were coming into the house, like a mixer, juicer, a new colour television, new curtains and cushions. Even the fridge was full of expensive cheese and foreign chocolates.

Though she never got the chance to ask her daughter from where she got the money, she nevertheless had a nagging suspicion. "What's your sister upto these days?" she asked her younger daughter one day.

"How am I supposed to know?" Rina retorted.

"You meet her more often than I do. Doesn't she tell you about her work?"

"I hardly get to talk to her. When I leave for college in the afternoons, she's either sleeping or has just woken up. We barely get the time to say hello," Rina explained. Radha would from time to time stuff some money into her hands. How did it matter to her what her sister did as long as some extra pocket money came her way.

One Sunday morning, while the trio were relaxing over their tea, Parvati looked up at Radha and said, "Radha, I want to talk to you."

"Yes amma, I've been meaning to talk to you too. I wanted to tell you that I'll be leaving next month. I've rented a room near Hauz Khas. It's small but good enough for me at the moment."

"I see." Pausing, Parvati asked, "Is Aloke moving in with you?"

"Aloke? But why should he?" asked Radha.

"He's your husband. Or how else will you pay the rent?"

"I don't need Aloke to pay the rent. As if he can without a job. I'll pay from my own earnings," Radha retorted.

"What earnings?"

"Never mind. I don't want to discuss it now. Maybe some other time," and with that Radha hurried out of the room, putting a stop to all enquiries.

Radha enjoyed her first taste of freedom. Freedom from her mother, her husband, her sister and even her friends. No prying questions, no explanations given. When her inquisitive landlord enquired about her status, she lied that her husband was working in the Gulf and, since she was busy with a project, they had agreed that she would stay back. That seemed to satisfy his curiosity though his wife asked her a few times as to why she did not publicise her married status by wearing a *mangalsutra* or vermillion in her parting. When Radha smiled it off, the landlord's wife just shrugged, "With these modern girls, it's hard to tell."

Gradually she started building bridges with her father. She also befriended Asha, much to Parvati's dismay. She knew that the easy way up the Delhi social ladder would be through them, permanent Page 3 fixtures. Sunil also realised his attractive daughter could be a boon to him too. Slowly he started handing out small responsibilities to her. Soon after, she started assisting Asha in editing Sunil's works. In the day she worked for her father and at night, for herself—Hari, Robin, Sanjay were just a few in the list of men who walked in and out of her life.

Aloke dropped in one morning. "How have you been?" he asked hesitantly.

"How do you see me?" Radha replied saucily.

"You look different. Not the Radha I knew."

"I am different now."

"So I've heard," Aloke said softly.

"And what have you heard?"

"Not very good things I'm afraid."

"Good or bad, you have no right to sermonise," she said sharply.

"I think I do, as legally you're still my wife and my name gets sullied in the process," said Aloke.

"In that case, let's get a divorce. You organise everything and I'll sign the papers. And don't worry, I won't retain your name. That's the last thing I want in any case."

A few months after the divorce, Aloke headed back home, where he got a job as a lecturer in a local college. Radha enjoyed being footloose and fancy-free. Most of her friends had settled down to marriage and kids and happy domesticity, but for Radha, at twenty-seven, life was one big party, and she enjoyed herself immensely.

However, it was difficult to ignore the little voice at the back of her mind. No husband, no family, no goal in life. Sometimes she wondered where she was headed. I cannot carry on like this. I'm wasting the best years of my life. At others, she revelled in her uncertainties. Let's take life as it comes. One day at a time.

Roger Smith came into her life soon after. They met at one of her father's readings. Roger was bowled over by the sultry beauty. He was heading the local British Council, one of the youngest chiefs the Council had in Delhi till date. The duo kept meeting—first for coffee, then for dinner at classy restaurants and finally at Roger's elegant apartment in Chanakyapuri, the very posh diplomatic enclave in Delhi.

After Aloke, it was Roger who left a deep impression on Radha's mind. Charming, understanding, sensitive to her needs, he was unlike all the men she had dated. For the first time, Radha also started enjoying sex, exploring newer avenues with him.

They became an item in Delhi society. During the Christmas holidays, Roger insisted she go home with him to Kent. Radha happily agreed. This was her first visit abroad. The cold notwithstanding, she enjoyed every bit of her stay in Kent.

Life continued well for the couple till one day Roger dropped a bomb—he was being transferred to Colombo. He wanted Radha to accompany him. "It's time we got married and settled down."

Radha was in a dilemma. She loved Roger, but did not want to commit to anyone. Not yet. She did not want to be strapped as the wife of a government officer. She had just had a taste of the glamour and wealth of upper-class Delhi society, which she was not keen to trade for obscure postings.

"Give me some time to think, darling. I'm not prepared for marriage yet. I'm sure you understand?"

"I do, honey. But my posting starts from June and I'll be leaving for Colombo next month. Perhaps, I'll leave you to think on your own for a while?"

Soon Roger left, but Radha stayed on. She was restless, however, and wanted to get out of the city. But where to, she was not sure. Six months had passed and Christmas was around the corner again. Roger called, "It's beautiful out here honey. You'll love Colombo. Just grab a bag and join me for Christmas–New Year week. We'll do some great things together, honey."

"Actually Roger I'd love to...but...

"No buts and ifs. I'm sending you a return ticket via Madras," Roger said with finality.

A few days later Radha was at the Madras airport, heading to the international terminal to board an Air Lanka flight to Colombo. She suddenly came face to face with someone who looked vaguely familiar. As recognition dawned, she smiled apprehensively, to which the gentleman gave a warm smile, a smile he specially reserved for attractive young ladies.

"Shravan *ji*, *namaste*," Radha folded her hands and smiled like one of those Air India hostesses. "You're such a superb actor," she continued in her charming lilt. "Oh, by the way, I'm Radha. Radha Pal. Sunil Pal's daughter."

"Of course, yes. I've heard of Sunil Pal. I have not had the good fortune to meet him yet. You write poems?"

"Not much. Just a little now and then. I am a dancer," Radha lied promptly, and it shocked her that she could do so with such a straight face. Of course, she'd learnt Bharata Natyam from the eminent *guru* Kuttyamma for twelve long years and had even had her *arangetram*. But that was years ago. She had never considered dance as a career option in all these years and she wondered why she had suddenly mentioned it. Was it to sound important or impressive?

It dawned on her just then that she had not had a steady career in all these years. Nor was she professionally qualified. The art she had perhaps the longest single association with was dance. Whatever the reason, she was pleased that she said so. And she suddenly realised that dance could be the answer to her restless spirit, the anchor which she had been seeking for sometime.

"So where you are going?" Shravan broke into her reverie.

"Colombo. And you?"

"Bombay. I just finished a shooting schedule in Madras. Back to home," he smiled boyishly. "You stay in Madras?"

"No. Delhi."

"You are going on holiday?" Shravan asked inquisitively. "Alone?"

"Not really. I've actually been invited for a seminar on modern dance," she said airily, beginning to enjoy this little game of deception.

"Oh, that is interesting," Shravan was impressed. He glanced at his watch and realised that if he dallied any longer with this pretty lady, he would miss his flight. "I will have to hurry. Otherwise I will miss my plane. It was nice talking to you Radha. Do you come to Bombay?"

"Sometimes, yes. I have family there in Colaba. Where do you stay?"

"Dadar. Five Gardens. Why don't I give you my card? My numbers are here. You call me when you are in Bombay next. We will catch up. Nice talking to you."

As he hurried towards the security check, he turned around several times to wave goodbye. Radha could see that he was totally charmed by her. She smiled to herself triumphantly and walked away.

Colombo was a charming old-fashioned city and Roger was a great host. He'd taken the week off so he took Radha to a nearby beach resort where they soaked in the sun, ate, drank and made love. She had a good time, but felt a nagging sense of restlessness throughout. She also noticed that Roger did not once mention marriage.

Radha thought about Bombay. The city of dreams. In fact, megadreams. And glamour. And wealth. She also thought about Shravan Singh and the way he had looked at her.

Shravan Singh was not particularly good-looking – in fact he was an inch shorter than her. Nor was he a movie star. A competent television actor, he had shot into the limelight recently because of some heart-rending performances. He was being tipped as the next superstar of television after Shekhar Suman.

Radha decided to take a chance. What do I have to lose? Maybe through Shravan Singh I can get a foothold in Bollywood, where all the money and fame is, she thought. To someone with no background in cinema, even a small-time actor like Shravan Singh was a hero.

"Alright then. Bombay, here I come."

Roger was surprised when Radha got her ticket re-routed to Bombay. "Got some work there?" he enquired.

"Not really. Just catching up with my cousins," Radha replied casually.

Meanwhile, Shravan had also thought of Radha a few times, wondering when she would come to Bombay. "Either that or I'll have to track her down through her father and surprise her." Shravan visited Delhi often as his parents lived there.

He did not have to wait long. One morning when he picked up the phone he was pleasantly surprised to hear Radha's voice. She spoke in chaste Hindi and this pleased Shravan as he had to struggle to speak correct English. They decided to meet.

One meeting led to another and another, till one night, Shravan booked them into one of those small motels in the suburbs which are rented by the hour, with no questions asked. The floodgates of their passion were thrown open. Thereafter there was no looking back.

The only hitch was the fact that Shravan was married with an eight-year-old daughter whom he was extremely fond of. Shravan's wife, Sushila, was his former classmate from college and they had married soon after they had graduated. Sushila had stood by Shravan during his early years as a struggling actor, working as a teacher to keep the house together and Shravan's dreams alive. After the birth of their daughter, Sia, she had quit her job to concentrate on home and hearth.

Casting was on full swing for a new film by a well-known director for whom Shravan had worked. "Can't I assist the choreographer? After all, I have trained in classical dance," Radha asked Shravan.

"Let's see, I'll ask him," Shravan shrugged. He not only asked the director, but begged and pleaded with him till he agreed. Shravan desperately needed Radha by his side.

Radha was quick to learn the tricks of the trade. With Shravan's contacts, she landed a few other offers, small-budget films, which honed her skills, gave her a steady income, and most of all ensured her stay in Mumbai. It was tough initially, to make headway in an industry, which was very feudal in its attitude. Her only "sugar daddy" was Shravan, and even he was too small a name to matter. She made contacts quickly, followed it up with professionalism and landed some contracts due to her own initiative.

Eventually, she established herself as an independent choreographer. Radha Pal had arrived—a sensuous classical dancer who believed in the purity of the dance form and yet was willing to experiment with new movements, for reasons which were "aesthetic rather than financial". But the money poured in nevertheless. A couple of years into mainstream Bollywood films, Radha became a better-known name in the industry than Shravan. She was often referred to as the "dusky dancer from Delhi".

Meanwhile, Shravan's career was going downhill. His overpowering passion for Radha had robbed him of clarity of thought. Tongues wagged and Sushila got wind of their affair. When she protested, Shravan ticked her off. He soon moved out of the house and started living with Radha. He missed his daughter, but alcohol and heart ruled his head and made her absence bearable.

Initially Radha enjoyed Shravan's attention and company, accompanying him to most film parties. Gradually, when she started making a name for herself, she went out less and less with Shravan. She did not want her name to be linked to a little-known actor. One day she gently told Shravan to return to his wife. "I think you've been unfair to Sushila and Sia. You must give your marriage another shot."

"Oh, really!" Shravan was taken aback. "What's happened to you? It took you so long to realise it? Why didn't you say so when I moved in with you?"

"I admit to being selfish then..." Radha replied but Shravan butted in.

"And since when did you decide to become Madam Selfless?" His voice rose in a scream, "Or has fame and money got into that pretty little head? You are already tired of me?"

At the end of it, Radha packed her bags and walked out of Shravan's life into that of the young and upcoming director, Sivanandan.

Inspite of phone calls from Shravan and numerous attempts at a reconciliation, Radha remained firm. In desperation, Shravan tried to reach out to Sushila, but she was too hurt to forgive and forget. She had earlier filed for divorce and refused to withdraw the petition. The court gave her the custody of their child. Shravan tried to kidnap his daughter unsuccessfully and was told by the court to behave himself.

Hurt and loneliness made him hit the bottle with a vengeance and for days together he refused to come out of his apartment. He sunk to an all-time low, physically, emotionally, and mentally. Radha had gone out of his life as suddenly as she had entered it. Sushila pulled herself together and continued her life with her daughter, letting time heal her scars. Inspite of her love for her father, Sia found it hard to forgive him for his behaviour towards them and this was the hardest blow for Shravan.

The excessive drinking took a toll on his health and he was forced to give up alcohol completely. Slowly he started picking up the threads of his life. He did bit roles as his health would not permit him to work for long hours. Without liquor to dull his senses, the road to reality was long and hard. With heartache and bitterness, Shravan Singh watched the rise of Radha Pal.

There would be the likes of Shravan in future—Sivanandan and then Steve Bunting the Caribbean cricketer whom she had seduced. Being Bunting's girlfriend not only gave her a calling card to the city's hotspots, but also fetched lucrative offers of dance shows abroad.

At times, she did feel bad. For Shravan, who had wrecked his marriage on account of her. But not once did she feel guilty. The word had no place in her emotional vocabulary. "I didn't want to marry them. They were attracted towards me and attraction doesn't always mean marriage. You win some, you lose some. But where are my friends? Have I been too hard on them?" she thought as she watched the fan whir. "Maybe. Maybe not. I don't know. Perhaps in my hurry to make it big, I have overlooked them. Or maybe the kind of life I am leading has distanced us. Or is it that they have deliberately distanced themselves from me? I am rich and famous now. The choreographer Radha Pal. Then where have my friends gone?"

Radha looked up and suddenly her eyes fell on the clock on the wall. It was ten to five.

"Oh shit. It's almost five. Rajan will be here any moment. Let me make myself a cup of coffee before that." The thought of the well-roasted coffee beans shook Radha out of her reverie. As well as her past.

THE PIANO TEACHER

"C'MON IN," MRS D'SOUZA BELLOWED, LOOKING up at her visitor as she put a playing card on the table, "Oh. It's you. So what's up now, Vincy?"

"Nothing Aunty. Just came to aks for a favour." Vincent Gomes stood with habitual awkwardness, fiddling with his shirt button.

"Now what?" Mrs D'Souza asked, almost anticipating his answer as she shifted her weight from one side of the armchair to the other.

"Small favour Aunty. I just wanted to borrow some money. It's month ending now. I'll give it by the fifth. Promise."

"Bollocks. You still owe me a hundred and fifty rupees from last month. Where do you think an old woman like me can afford to squander away precious money? Look at me, even at seventy-nine I have to give piano lessons to make ends meet. Look at you youngsters. Why don't you work hard?" Mrs D'Souza said as she heaved herself up from the armchair. "How much now?"

"Just two hundred rupees. Promise I'll return this—plus a hundred and fifty next month. I'm working hard Aunty, but my luck is not good," Vincy said, with his Anglo-Indian lilt.

"What do you mean by 'luck is not good'?" Mrs D'Souza mimicked, adding, "How come Rafiq who works in the same theatre as you is earning more?"

"You don't understand Aunty. We're upstairs, ushering people, showing them their seats. Rafiq is downstairs, getting his cut from the black guys men."

"Black guys? Who on earth are these black guys?" Mrs D'Souza asked.

"Those fellas, men, who black tickets. Them selling hundred rupees for two hundred, sometimes three hundred. Those fellas give Rafiq sometimes forty-fifty rupees cut on one ticket men. Otherwise he not allowing them to stand in front of gate and sell double price, triple price ticket. Rafiq..."

"Okay, okay. Here. I can spare only hundred rupees now. It's month ending for me too. And don't forget to return two hundred and fifty rupees next month," Mrs D'Souza cut Vincy short.

"You don't have to aks, Aunty. I'll return it. You know how expensive vejtbles, men. Got hungry mouths to feed." Vincy said as he made his way towards the landing.

"And one more thing, sonny," Mrs D'Souza said after him. "Remember, honesty is the best policy. Don't ever get into such rackets like Rafiq."

Though Vincy was a little slow on the uptake, Valerie D'Souza felt sorry for him. He, his wife, Rachel, and son, Columbus, lived with his brother Ashley and his family in a ground floor apartment of their building Maryam Manzil. Ashley was a cleaner in a cargo liner and was out on the sea for three to four months at a stretch. The one-bedroom, all of 550 sq. feet apartment, housed him, his wife Judy, his daughters Roxanne and Joanne and, of course, Vincy's family.

While Ashley earned anything between forty to fifty thousand rupees a month, Vincy subsisted on a mere three thousand rupees as an usher in Cinetime theatre. Though the former had a two-bedroom apartment of his own down the road, he refused to move his family there for fear of losing his share of the ancestral house. He even insisted that Vincy share the household expenses equally.

They alternated paying the electricity and water bills. The wives cooked separately in the same tiny kitchen, squabbling most of the time. When it was Vincy's turn to pay the electricity bill, he and his wife would follow Ashley and his family around the house, switching off the lights and fan every time someone left the room. It was a hilarious sight! Every time the television or music system was on, Vincy could be heard complaining about the tremendous waste of electricity. However, when it was Ashley's turn to foot the bill, Vincy and Rachel would have the TV set on throughout the day and almost half the night.

Almost always, Vincy would be broke by the end of the month. He would borrow from neighbours and friends, whose predicament was almost equal to, if not worse, than his.

Mrs D'Souza was not much better off. She made two to three thousand rupees a month from her piano tuitions. Luckily for her, her late husband's pension of four thousand rupees came in handy each month. "Had it not been for Walter's army pension, God knows how I would have survived. I would have had to swallow my pride and beg from Jason and Anne," Mrs D'Souza said to herself.

Her son Jason lived with his family near Sydney, while her daughter Anne lived with her husband in Delhi. Neither bothered to visit her or even call her up except to wish her every Christmas. "If you ever need anything, just buzz me Mummy," Anne would say once in a way, but Valerie knew she did not mean a word of it.

Never mind. Such is life. Atleast I have some well-meaning friends and students who care for me, Mrs D'Souza thought as she ate a banana and washed it down with a bowl of curd. It was almost ten o'clock, nearly three hours after her breakfast of tea, toast and fried bacon. Time now for her first student for the day to arrive, and she always liked to give lessons on a full stomach.

"Thumb on Middle C," Mrs D'Souza pointed to the key with her walking stick. Natasha placed her thumb on the key—a tall, slim and attractive lady in her late thirties who had just started learning to play the piano. This was her fourth lesson.

She was her newest pupil and Mrs D'Souza wondered how long she would last.

She had had many students like Natasha Singh. Rich, bored housewives with more money than they could spend. With her husband in office and son at school and servants to look after the house, Natasha had the whole day to herself. Mornings were usually spent in the gym or the beauty parlour. Then it was lunch dates or kitty parties with girlfriends or catching a quick matinee show at the nearby multiplex. By early evening she would be home, either instructing the cook on the dinner menu or advising the nanny on how to look after her son.

With so much time on her hands, Natasha felt like doing something constructive. Like learning to play an instrument, maybe the piano. She found it soothing to the ears. More importantly, it would increase her social standing. She visualised herself playing at parties and her husbands' colleagues looking on in wonder, ("Wow! How come we didn't know all these years that Keval has such a talented wife.") while their wives glared at her with jealousy and false smiles of appreciation.

"Why don't you just teach me to play a few pieces Mrs D'Souza," Natasha asked.

"If you cannot read music and don't know your basic notes, just playing a few pieces from memory won't do you any good, my girl. What's the point in taking lessons then?"

"Because I love music," Natasha cooed.

Bollocks, thought Mrs D'Souza, but she did not say so. Instead she said, "Then learn to be patient my dear and things will be clear to you soon. Now play the space notes of the treble clef."

Natasha Singh pressed the F and A and C and E keys.

"Good. Now play the line notes of the bass clef."

The slim well-manicured fingers, flashing with diamonds, hit G and B and D and F and A.

"That's right my dear. Now play EGBDF."

As Valerie D'Souza played Patience and absentmindedly watched television, she suddenly saw a tiny rat scurrying across the kitchen. Hers was a tiny one-room-kitchen flat, with a dingy bathroom attached to it. Too small to even house her meagre belongings. But then, this was all she could afford and with a rent as low as rupees two thousand a month, she had no reason to complain.

"I'll have to get Mr Kichlu to help me sort out my things someday soon," she said to herself. But she liked to postpone such work. Anything which made her move around too much was not welcome. Mr Kichlu's repeated cajoling always fell on deaf ears.

"Why don't you walk around the building atleast, Mrs D'Souza? You will feel a lot better. Look at the amount of weight you have put on. You will end up with a stroke one of these days."

"How does it matter one way or the other Mr Kichlu? I'm almost eighty. My children don't care for me. I've lived life and seen good days with Walter. What do I have to look forward to now? At least let me enjoy my last years, eating and lazing around. Whether I diet or exercise, I'll have to go one of these days. So I might as well live it up. What d'you say, Mr Kichlu?" The memory of that conversation made her laugh.

The ring of the doorbell broke into her thoughts.

"C'mon in, Doel," she bellowed in her typical style, anticipating her latest entrant as she looked up at the wall-clock. She noticed the cobwebs beneath it, "I must remember to tell the *bai* to clean it when she comes." It was eleven thirty. Doel Bose had been coming at this time, thrice a week for the past two years. Mondays, Wednesdays and Fridays. Initially it used to be for an hour each day, then it gradually increased to a couple of hours and nowadays to a good four hours. Doel would be here till four.

Doel didn't just play the piano for those four hours. In fact, piano was not so much a priority on their agenda these days. Chatting and having lunch or tea together was what they enjoyed most. Doel was one of those matronly, well-settled housewives who arrive at a complacency in life before they reach thirty. Having sent off her husband to work with a heavy lunch, and having dropped her son to school, she had the whole afternoon to herself.

Bored and wanting to occupy herself, she had stumbled upon Mrs D'Souza's name at a friend's, whose son was learning to play the piano from the old lady. "She's a good teacher," her friend told her. "And very patient with her students."

"But am I not too old for it?" Doel had asked.

"She has students older than you."

Doel nodded at this. She remembered that as a child she had dabbled in music lessons, erratically. She thought she could take it up more seriously now. After convincing her husband to allow her to take lessons, she had got the old family piano tuned. And had embarked on her journey.

During the first few months she was quite serious. After dropping her son at school, she would turn up at Mrs D'Souza's for her lessons. After returning home, she had lunch and with great difficulty would forego afternoon siesta to practise on the piano, till Diptosh returned from school. Then the humdrum of daily existence and her dual roles of mother and wife took over.

Seeing how sincere she was, Mrs D'Souza grew quite fond of her. Fondness resulted in friendship, as they both reached out to each other, sharing a certain loneliness. Their common passion was food. The three days that Doel came for her classes, Mrs D'Souza did not have to make lunch. Doel brought a hot case full of scrumptious Bengali delicacies like mustard fish-*macher jhol*, fishhead with *dal* and boiled rice with generous dollops of clarified butter.

In return, Mrs D'Souza usually brought out remnants of an earlier meal from the fridge—sausage curry or pork vindaloo or mutton stew or some such Goan preparation. While she cleaned her plate of Doel's fish curry and rice, Doel would wipe the remains of a delicious mutton stew with a piece of garlic bread.

Lunch over, the two usually enjoyed a cosy chit-chat.

"How's Sadaf? Haven't seen her in a while. Has she been coming for her lessons?" Doel asked today, settling herself comfortably in the sofa.

"Where has she been coming? It's been over a month since I last saw her. Hasn't even bothered to call," Mrs D'Souza replied, stretching herself on the divan which doubled as a bed at night.

"And how's Ajay?" Doel asked.

"Oh, he's fine," Mrs D'Souza said absently. "Try and get Star Sports. Let's catch up with the cricket scores."

"Is Sadaf still pursuing Ajay?" Doel smiled as she flipped through the channels.

"Oh. We're in a miserable state. Tendulkar's gone. Fat chance of winning. Looks like these Zimbabweans will beat us hollow today," Mrs D'Souza said. "Huh... what did you ask? Yes, yes, about Sadaf and Ajay. Well, I think she's cooled towards him. There's a new man in her life."

"Really!"

"Yep. And guess what? She's never seen him. Just fell for his voice over the phone. He's a Pakistani, I believe. Stays in Karachi. Sadaf's in seventh heaven these days."

"Silly girl. How can you fall for someone you've not met."

Both of them loved these moments when they made small talk, with the television running. Sometimes they sat together in companionable silence. Without a care in the world. Occasionally they fell asleep only to be woken by the ringing of the bell. For on the dot at four, old Mr Kichlu would be at the door, with his familiar toothless smile and, "Good evening Mrs D'Souza. Good evening, Miss Bose."

Why he insisted on calling Doel Miss instead of Mrs remained an eternal mystery to Valerie. When Mr Kichlu arrived, Doel picked herself up, hastily ran a comb through her hair, dabbed some lipstick and headed towards the door.

"Alright then. See you day after Mrs D'Souza. See you Mr Kichlu. Take care you two. I'll have to rush and pick up Diptosh from school. Bye."

"Bye," they chorused.

Valerie D' Souza ambled into the kitchen while Mr Kichlu picked up the newspaper. In between he made a comment or asked Mrs D'Souza for her opinion on a particular topic.

"Terrible. The underworld connection these filmstars have."

"Yes, I know. Dreadful." She placed a cup of piping hot tea and a plate of savouries for him. "We have a small-time producer living upstairs. He has all sorts of strange-looking people coming to see him. We're scared there may be a shootout someday. I sometimes hear him arguing loudly with his visitors. God knows what he's up to."

Mrs D'Souza felt sorry for Mr Kichlu. Her sympathies were, however, not without a tinge of anger. The biggest blunder Mr Kichlu had committed in his youth was to sleep with his secretary, Rosy. Rosy became pregnant, though he was never quite sure whether the baby was his or not. When Mrs Kichlu learnt about it, she was livid. She threw Mr Kichlu out of the house and started divorce proceedings against him. Mrs Kichlu got to keep the bungalow whilst Mr Kichlu got to keep Rosy and another man's baby.

Mr Kichlu bought a small apartment for himself and Rosy, who subsequently became Mrs Kichlu No. 2, and for her daughter, Tulip. Rosy was a good thirty years younger than Mr Kichlu and soon got bored with her "old man". The fur flew and, with age, Mr Kichlu became more tolerant of Rosy's tantrums.

Now at eighty-two, he was too weak to protest against the ill-treatment meted out to him by his wife and daughter. He was told to leave the house by nine in the morning and not return before nine in the evening. "Be grateful man I'm letting you stay. It's enough man I have to tolerate you during nights. At least let me have some peace during the day you old bugger," Rosy would scream.

"But this is my house," Mr Kichlu tried to put up a feeble protest.

"Shut up you old fool. If you can give No. 1 the bungalow man, don't I deserve this for tolerating you old bugger."

"But..."

"Just get out man, before I whack you," Rosy would say viciously.

All he was given was a bucket of water to bathe and clean himself and a cup of tea and stale chappatis or bread for breakfast. Though all his earthly belongings could fit into a small bag, which was kept in the corridor along with his rolled up bedding, Mr Kichlu always turned up neatly dressed, in a pair of freshly ironed trousers and shirt.

His first round would be to his old bungalow at Bandra, where Mrs Kichlu No. 1 stayed. The mornings were spent doing odd errands for her, like paying the electricity or telephone bills and buying vegetables and sundry items from the market. In return she fed him lunch and let him sit around the house during the mornings and watch television. The odd cup of tea was sometimes thrown in if she was in a generous mood.

"So how's your Rosy darling?" Mrs Kichlu No. 1 would ask mockingly.

"Please, Sarita. I don't want to think of her now."

"I was just being polite," Sarita would shrug, reminding him of his foolishness so many years back.

Post-lunch, Mr Kichlu would take the No. 56 bus from Pali Hill to Lokhandwala. He would get off at the stop at the head of the lane and walk the few furlongs to Maryam Manzil. Tea and an early supper was what he looked forward to at Mrs D'Souza's. He also enjoyed catching up with some of her students, especially Mr Banerjee, with whom he would exchange tips on racing.

Mr Kichlu and Walter D'Souza had been friends in the old days. After Walter's death, Mr Kichlu visited Mrs D'Souza often, as she suffered from bouts of depression. In order to combat her loneliness, she insisted Mr Kichlu have tea with her every evening.

"I'm sure Rosy won't mind. Tell her you're with me. In fact, bring her over sometimes," Mrs D'Souza told him.

"You don't worry about that. Rosy's too busy with her life. She doesn't miss me much these days."

So the daily ritual of having tea together began. It was much later that Mrs D'Souza found out that the tea and little savouries she served him was his dinner. He never got any food to eat at home. He would wander in the streets till nine o'clock and return home to do the odd chores and sleep. Often his stomach would rumble in his sleep. It was Mrs D'Souza who first suggested that he stay on longer and have dinner before returning home.

"No, no, Mrs D'Souza. I do not want to inconvenience you," he had initially tried to protest.

"Bollocks. It will be no inconvenience. As it is there is always a lot of food left. It'll be nice to eat with you. I get lonely in the evenings at times."

After her last student left after eight o'clock, Mrs D'Souza and Mr Kichlu would have dinner together. Sometimes she would grill a sandwich with Laughing Cow Cheese. At other times she would order food from the nearby Guru Da Dhaba, which served wholesome vegetarian fare at very reasonable rates. The high point were the hot chappatis, which they both relished

"Somehow I could never get my chappatis this round," Mrs D'Souza would say while breaking off a bite of the chappati. Very often they had what remained from lunch.

"Ah this is delicious...this fish curry," Mr Kichlu asked. "What fish is this?"

"It's called rohu."

"Rohu? I've never heard of it."

"It's a fresh water fish which the Bengalis normally eat. Doel got it from home," Mrs D'Souza explained.

"Did she get the fish from Calcutta?"

"No, Mr Kichlu. You do get it in Bombay. It's available at Char Bangla market."

"How come I've never heard of it before?"

"That's because of that girl you picked up for a wife. She has no background to speak of. I'm sure she's not had any other fish except those dried Bombay ducks."

Mr Kichlu did not say anything.

Usually around nine, he would leave Maryam Manzil and take a leisurely walk home, through the Lokhandwala main road, admiring the prettily lit shop windows. There were lots of things which he felt like buying, but Mr Kichlu realised that he had little need for material goods. After all, his days were numbered. So where was the need to hoard? Live for the present. Spend whatever little money that was left on things that really give you pleasure, even if it is momentary, Mr Kichlu thought to himself. Things like food. Or the races. Ah, the races, Mr Kichlu smiled as he thought about it.

On Saturdays and Sundays he would be at the races with a hundred rupees or so in his pocket which he almost always lost. This was preceded by the Friday evening spats he had with Mrs D'Souza over the fifty rupees he took from her to go to the races. The entry fee was as low as twelve rupees and the betting could even start at ten rupees. But since Mr Kichlu had seen better days, he insisted on betting with whatever money he had left. Sometimes it would be fifty rupees, sometimes a hundred.

"I don't mind giving you money for food or other essentials Mr Kichlu. But for heaven's sake, why the races? You know you lose, so why do you want to pour precious money down the drain?" Mrs D'Souza told him angrily.

"I don't care if I lose. I enjoy going to the races, it makes me happy. Why grudge me my happiness Mrs D'Souza? Besides, it's my money. So let me spend it as I like," Mr Kichlu said stubbornly.

He was right. Why grudge him his happiness? After grumbling a bit, Mrs D'Souza would eventually give in. Mr Kichlu's sister in Delhi would send Mrs D'Souza a money order of five hundred rupees every month as pocket money for her brother. She was advised to give it to him in small measures, as his sister was aware of his penchant for gambling it away.

Mr Kichlu lost more and more money at the races. Mrs D'Souza got angrier every time he lost. Finally Mr Kichlu stopped confiding in her if he lost money. However, his sheepish expression on Monday afternoons gave him away. She figured out the previous day's developments from his looks.

"He'll never learn," she would complain to Doel. "I get angry the way he wastes his little savings."

"What to do, Mrs D'Souza. I guess it gives him pleasure."

"I guess so. That's why I've stopped arguing with him now. Let him enjoy his last few days just the way he likes it. The rest I leave to God."

"Good," Mrs D'Souza noted. "Now play the D Major scale." Jeet obliged.

"Practise the finger drills my boy," Mrs. D'Souza told one of her favourite pupils.

She seldom had any problems with him. At twelve, he was far too serious for his age. He excelled in his studies and had been earning distinctions in the last three grade examinations of the Trinity College of Music, London. He was an obedient and polite child and simply adorable. He reminded her of Jason at his age. How Walter would admonish him for clinging to her. "You don't want to be a mama's boy, son, do you?" Walter would say. Mrs D'Souza smiled at the recollection.

Now look, how far away he has gone, physically and emotionally. Too busy with his wife and children, no time for his old mother. How right the old saying is—a son is a son until he gets a wife.

"Yes. Yes. I Know Mr Banerjee...But what to do...No. No. She won't listen. No point..." Mr Kichlu's voice cut into Mrs D'Souza's thoughts.

"Lower your volume, Mr Kichlu, will you? You're breaking Jeet's concentration. Why don't you take the handset into the kitchen?"

This was nothing new. Everyday Mr Kichlu made his calls to his old friends and would talk incessantly. Every now and then his voice would rise in excitement and she would have to tell him to be softer. He would oblige for a few minutes, but would lapse to his loud-voiced banter. No point. Mr Kichlu will never change, Mrs D'Souza thought. I cannot be firmer than this or else he will sulk for the rest of the evening and make my life miserable.

"Do you think Zimbabwe will beat us?" Mr Kichlu asked while watching television. Jeet had just left and Mrs D'Souza wanted to catch up on the score before her next student came in. Arman Arora, at six, was one of her youngest students and a thoroughly spoilt brat. Mrs D'Souza wasn't quite enthusiastic about him, but her responsibility as a teacher forbade her from making any such distinctions.

"Oh God! That brat will bang my keys so hard that he'll spoil them again. I just got them repaired yesterday," she muttered to herself.

"What Mrs D'Souza?" Mr Kichlu enquired.

"No. Nothing. I was just talking to myself. Did you say something?"

"Yes. I was wondering whether Zimbabwe will beat us or not."

"Beat us! They've already done so. We're nearly done in. Not a chance of winning now." Just then the bell rang. Without turning from the television she bellowed, "C'mon in Arman." Now I will have to put up with this brat for some time, she thought. Look at the things one has to do in one's old age just to make ends meet.

"So, young man, have you practised your lessons?" she enquired.

Arman never spoke or answered her. He only smiled back, in a flash of blackened and chipped teeth. The result of too many chocolates. His vacuous smile irritated Mrs D'Souza even more.

"Why don't you answer? How can I teach you if you just keep smiling and never answer? C'mon now, play the Happy Birthday song," she said, annoyed. Just then Arman's mother, Amisha entered.

"Good evening Aunty," she smiled, then looking at Mr Kichlu added, "Good evening Uncle." When she had settled down, Mrs D'Souza turned to her, "So, Madam... When are you going to start your lessons?"

"Soon, Aunty."

"And how soon is that soon of yours? It's been six months since you decided to learn the piano."

"I know. But what to do. I don't get enough time. Akash is so busy with his films you know," Amisha said sheepishly. Her husband Akash Arora was one of the better-known music directors in the Hindi film industry.

Her reason for not learning the piano was quite strange. If Akash was busy, what did it have to do with her? But Mrs D'Souza knew quite well that it was an excuse for the idle rich. She knew better than to ask.

Mrs D'Souza's heart skipped a beat. Arman had just started hammering the keys on her piano in an attempt to play *Happy Birthday*. It made no difference to him if she told him not to. His parents never disciplined him and so Arman was not used to obeying orders.

"Amisha, I was just wondering, wouldn't it be wise to give Arman a break from his piano lessons for a while. Maybe for a year or so. He can start after that, when he's more mature," Mrs D'Souza casually said.

"But Aunty, he must learn the piano. It is an important instrument."

"I know. But he's too young. Besides, he is already learning the tabla and the sarod. I think by learning too many instruments at a time, he is losing his concentration."

"But he must know how to play all these instruments. Or else how will he be a music director like his father. The tradition has to continue." Amisha sounded important.

"Don't be silly, my girl. He is only a child. He has all the years ahead to learn. Let him enjoy his childhood."

"Oh, don't worry, Aunty. He's got his whole life to have fun. Let him learn now. He can manage different instruments at a time. After all, it is in his genes."

Bollocks, thought Mrs D'Souza. But no point wasting your energy in pointless talk. Let Arman fool around. Let his parents pay. If they don't mind throwing their money, then why should I bother?

After dinner Mr Kichlu would get up and say, "Alright Mrs D'Souza, thank you very much. Good night and take care of yourself. I'll see you tomorrow." This was Mr Kichlu's standard goodbye. He had a long evening ahead. Once he reached home, he had to iron the clothes and then wait till Rosy and Tulip finished dinner, which was seldom before midnight. He would then do the dishes, roll out his bedding in the kitchen and lull himself to sleep.

What a life. When would it end? Mr Kichlu wondered. He knew Rosy and Tulip were waiting for him to die. He was equally stubborn and took a wicked pleasure by not giving in. For each day that he defied death, Rosy's misery increased, and seeing her unhappy made his life seem less miserable.

"Good night Mr Kichlu. And God bless," Mrs D'Souza replied. She too had a long night ahead. She seemed to sleep less and less each day. There were nights when she lay awake till the wee hours of the morning and was up again at the crack of dawn.

All sorts of thoughts niggled her. Some of her regular students were dropping out. The new ones were not consistent. Except for a few, most of her students did not even pay her on time. Sometimes they would even forget to pay and Mrs D'Souza would have to gently remind them. She hated doing this. It made her feel like a beggar. Some of them decided to only pay her for the months they came for their classes. If they took a month or two off in between, they did not even have the decency to offer her her fees.

Like Arman. Every few months, he would travel with his father on concert tours. Amisha never paid Mrs D'Souza when Arman absented himself. "I wonder if Arman will be able to continue his studies if he followed the same pattern in school," Mrs D'Souza complained to Doel.

"What to do Mrs D'Souza. Amisha is penny-wise, pound-foolish. How much richer can you get by pinching a few pennies from a poor woman? I've noticed that people with a lot of money have less value for others' money," Doel would say.

It worried her whether she would be able to manage with Walter's pension alone if she gave up her tuitions. Once in a while Jason would tell her to come and live with his family. At times when her monetary condition would reach an abysmal low, she would consider his offer seriously. But she knew that she would never be able to get along with her daughter-in-law, Padmini. "Who wants to be with that bitch?" she would tell Mr Kichlu. Besides, I am too used to this city to want to settle anywhere else, she thought.

They say that youth lives on hope while old age lives on memories. In the case of Valerie D'Souza it was a bit of both. Fond memories of her youth, happy days as Walter's wife and as a mother raising her two children. There were good times and bad, but they had managed as one happy family.

Now pushing eighty, at the fag end of her life, there was one hope she clung to, a hope that refused to die. A hope which she cherished, in spite of her bouts of insomnia, her obesity, high blood pressure, indifferent children and erratic students.

"I hope Ajay returns my money soon," she said loudly to herself. She had grown ill thinking about it. Ajay, a struggling young filmmaker, had borrowed three lakh rupees from her almost six years ago. He had spent it all shooting a pilot for a weekly television soap. He had seemed sincere and, in a rash moment, Mrs D'Souza had lent him all her savings in the hope that he would make it big someday. He had also promised to credit her as the producer. Valerie D'Souza secretly nurtured the hope of seeing the words PRODUCED BY: **VALERIE D'SOUZA** on the television screen when the credits rolled on. How would her neighbours and friends react to her sudden celebrity status. With bloody envy, she said to herself.

But that was not to be. The pilot was shunted from one channel to another and rejected by all. Now it lay languishing in her cupboard—all her life's savings in a single VHS tape.

She had dreamt of a small apartment for herself—with a kitchen where she could display her crockery and a studio where she could exhibit Walter's curios.

All her hopes of owning a small studio apartment lay reduced to the size of an eight by four inch tape. Had she invested the money in her bank, it would have doubled with interest by now. How could she blame Mr Kichlu? She had gambled away her life's savings too.

And all because of Ajay. Young and sincere and motivated Ajay. Her ex-student, diligent and endearing. Ajay. Who reminded her so much of her Jason when he was that age. Full of hope and ambition. Full of the future.

He had initially promised to return the money in a few months' time. Months turned to years and now it was nearly six years since she had last seen her money. Hope. That is all I have to live for. Hope and a positive spirit.

Was that a knock on the door?

"Who's that now? C'mon in, the door's open."

"It's me Aunty. I came to aks for something." Vincy entered sheepishly.

"Now what? I don't have any more money."

"No. I haven't come to aks for money. Rachel sends me to aks for two onions. These women, men, I tell you. All day sitting at home and watching TV. Now she's cooking *batata bhaji* for dinner and have no onions, men."

"Cooking dinner? Now? Look at the time. It's half-past ten. When will she finish and when will you eat?" Mrs D'Souza sighed as she went into the kitchen to fetch the two onions.

"We're used to eating late Aunty. Sometimes twelve, twelve-turty."

"Bad for the kids," Mrs D'Souza shrugged. "Here take these and run along." She handed the onions to Vincy. "I'm going to bed now. So don't come and ring my bell again."

"I promise, I won't. Tank you. Good night Aunty."

"Good night and God bless, my son."

I hope I don't have to see his face first thing in the morning tomorrow, 'aks-ing' me for something or the other, Valerie D'Souza muttered to herself as she latched the door and got ready to face another long night.

Waiting...

Promit kept waiting...

But Nita never turned up at the bus stop as promised. He had been waiting for forty minutes. She had promised to be here forty minutes back. "I'll be there at twelve sharp," she had told him over the phone the previous evening. "I can just about manage an hour between my coaching classes and returning home for lunch. So be there at twelve. At least we will get to spend an hour with each other."

No way she will come now because then she will never be able to make it home in time. Promit took one last longing look at his watch. *And she cannot risk making her folks angry, which is bound to be the case if they got to know she was seeing me secretly.* Rather dejectedly, he walked back towards his hostel. *Back to the grind now till Saturday next. One whole week. Seven more days. 24 X 7 hours. And endless minutes and seconds.... Shit. Why the hell didn't she have tuition classes every day? Atleast then I wouldn't* have to wait the whole week to see Nita for a measly hour. So much to say and so little time. It has been over a year since we have been meeting in secret and honestly it is getting us nowhere. I wonder if she feels the same way as I do about her. Well, she doesn't show it even if she does. But why the hell would she be meeting me like this if she were not serious about me. I'll ask her the next time we meet....

Nita sat in her room, waiting...

Promit was in the drawing room talking to her parents. It was a sensitive topic he would broach to them. His decision to marry Nita—rather their mutual decision. Seven years of discreet Saturday meetings had elapsed. And in those years, Nita had completed her secondary and then higher secondary education and, more recently, her graduation, with honours in History from Calcutta University. Now her parents were looking with great gusto for a suitable boy for her to marry. When she discussed this with Promit, they decided that it was time he met her parents and asked for her hand. After all, he had just landed a decent job with ICL, those computer people. And his future prospects looked bright, with a possible transfer to Australia, where the company headquarters was. Didn't he have a brilliant track record—a first class Masters in Economics, a diploma in computers and an MBA degree to boot? "Quite a catch," Nita remembered her sister Sutapa saying.

But the question was, would her parents think the same way. Even if Promit fit their bill of a suitable groom, her parents would still say no. They would explain that they could not agree as the boy was not of their choice. Never mind the eligibility quotient, Promit was their daughter's choice. And children these days are apt to be hasty in choosing their life partners. Nita parted the curtain gently and tried to strain her ears towards the drawing room. The decibels were of normal range. No heated exchanges. She looked at Sutapa and smiled.

Maybe her parents would consent. The eligibility quotient might have won. Or was it merely a lull before a violent storm? Nita knew Ma was keen she marry the Sens' younger son Ranajoy. Ma had always found Ranajoy dashing and thought they would make a handsome pair. Nita thought him an arrogant prig. What would her mother say of Promit now? Dark. Pimply. Skinny. Looks perpetually ill. How can my beauty marry him? Imagine what my grandchildren would look like if they took after their father...?

Promit stood waiting, beads of sweat running down his neck...

Dressed in an elaborate *dhoti* and *kurta* and *topor*—the thermocol headgear all Bengali bridegrooms are subjected to—Promit looked every inch the nervous bridegroom as he stood in the wedding *mandap*. Nita was yet to arrive and

Promit knew all eyes were rivetted on him. "Couldn't the Ghoshes find a better-looking boy for their daughter?" Promit heard a matronly woman tell another, as they perspired in their Benarasi silk saris in the middle of May. She was obviously a relative or friend of Nita's family. "His face resembles *Banglar paanch*," Promit heard another of her relatives say. *Banglar paanch* meaning a Bengali owl.

Suddenly there was a small commotion at one end of the ceremonial hall and all eyes turned. A few of Nita's male cousins were escorting her to the mandap, her father following close behind.

Am I not lucky to have her as my wife? She is indeed so pretty. Everyone is right. She is wasted on me. But never mind, all tongues will stop wagging once she takes the **pheras.** *Then she will be mine and mine alone. My trophy. I will show her off to all those who have made fun of my appearance.* Promit touched his hair, as if trying to assure himself that all this was for real. That he was not dreaming. *I hope this ordeal is over soon....*

Nita was dressed and waiting...

Why is Promit taking such a long time? She took a good look at herself in the mirror as she adjusted her sari. A lovely pink *tanchoi* with delicate silver leaf motifs. It set off her fair skin. Her college friends, Sunita, Mousumi and Kajal had pooled in to gift it to her on her wedding. She looked out of her apartment window towards the Sydney Harbour in the distance. She craned her neck towards the driveway downstairs, hoping to catch a glimpse of Promit's car.

Maybe he has been caught in the traffic. Or in the office? Should I call up and check? Forget it. He should be coming any moment now. He is aware of the cocktail at the Barts'. Oooh. I am excited. I love meeting people, especially these Australians. They are quite a charming lot. **Nita smiled.** *Especially when these white men ogle at me. I must seem so damn exotic to them. I love the way their women look at me too. Admiring my Indian clothes and going gaga over the fabric. And Promit looks so proud. I can see it in his eyes.* She kept smiling.

Gosh! Sydney. Australia. What a fabulous place to be in. I cannot believe it is true. That I am here. Far from the **gallis** *of Calcutta. Wonder what Sunita, Mousumi and Kajal are doing now? I wish they could see me in their sari. I wish Sutapa was here too. Oh, how I miss her. I hope she is able to come after her exams in February. I must tell Promit to book her ticket. I cannot wait for her to be here—I am going to take her around. Just Promit, Sutapa and me. Maybe we will ask Promit's friend Mihir to come along with us. Who knows? Something may just click between Mihir and Sutapa. He is quite a catch. And nice-looking too.* **Nita smiled.** *Oh, so typical of me. I should not be building castles in the air. Let's wait and see....*

Promit paced up and down the corridor, anxiously waiting...

Nita was in labour and her cries of pain both alarmed and disturbed him. Unable to bear it, he stepped out for a while. Mihir had come along to keep him company. He kept assuring Promit that it was all very normal and that he should stop worrying about Nita. "She will be fine. Just the regular procedure," Mihir said. "I know," Promit replied, "but I feel guilty she has to go through all that pain alone." "Just take it easy." Mihir put a hand on his shoulder.

But there was no stemming the anxiety of the first-time father. *I just hope Nita is able to pull through. What worries me is that she is going to deliver twins. Atleast that is what the doctor had said after the sonography. Only he did not mention the sex of the foetus. But to have twins first time round is going to be a doubly difficult task.* He gestured that he would he going out to Mihir. *I think I will have a smoke. I am nervous and exhausted. I just hope Nita is able to manage....*

Nita was irritable as she kept looking at her watch, waiting......

"Every time he does this to me. Tells me to get ready early and keeps me waiting. Work, office, work. That is all he can think of these days," her voice came loud and angry. "Oh for god's sake you two," she suddenly turned to her nine-year-old twins, Rumki and Jhumki. "Lower the volume or I will switch off the TV."

"Okay Ma," Jhumki said as Rumki picked up the remote and pressed down the volume button.

"That is better," Nita smiled. "Sorry about that girls. But I am a little tense, you see. The film will start in twenty minutes and it will take us atleast half an hour to reach the theatre. And look, your father has not yet come to pick me up."

"Call him and tell him *na*," Jhumki said.

"He has switched off his cell. No point now. We will be late anyway."

"I don't understand why you take this nonsense from Baba all the time. Every time he is late and every time you two get into a bad mood and miss the beginning of the film. Why don't you just go for a film with Sutapa *mashi* instead? Or Aunty Naina," Rumki piped up.

"Oh, be quiet. You won't understand," Nita said. The twins just shrugged and continued to watch *Tweenies*.

Gosh, how Promit has changed over the past decade. Earlier he used to fawn and fuss over her. Take her dutifully to the theatre for films and to posh restaurants for dinner. Now she had to virtually plead with him to take her out. He always complained of work, work and work. Either he was out of station on business tours for most of the month or else holed up in office, working late hours. Did he not care for his family?

Atleast he took the girls every Sunday morning to the club for a swim while she cooked the family's favourite meals. Sunday was the only day the family had lunch together, therefore it had to be elaborate. Shorshe illish or prawn malai curry. How I pamper his taste buds.

But he hardly bothers about my feelings. Here take this money and buy something for yourself. Sorry I could not get you anything from Paris.

Too busy. Why don't you buy yourself something with this money, is all he says these days. Money, money, money. That is all that seems to interest him. We already have enough. Why does he want more? I would rather have the romantic Promit of old than this corporate busybody. Nita looked at her watch. *Shit, we will miss this film too.*

Nita shrugged resignedly. *We have been missing out on the best years of our lives. On love. What is the point in having so much money if your husband has no affection for you? It has been ages since Promit made love to me last....* A tear rolled down Nita's cheek.

In the lobby of the oncologist's clinic, Promit kept waiting...

Nita was undergoing her check-up inside. "Shit," Promit looked at his watch. "I am getting late for the meeting. I wonder how much longer it will take? At this rate, I will never be able to make it to the cocktail at the Hyatt. And Cheryl will be disappointed. She was clearly looking forward to it."

Nita had not been keeping well for some months now and had been complaining of stomach aches and headaches. In the past month, her stomach had bloated unusually. Promit had casually asked her to get a check-up done but Nita hated visits to doctors. She ignored it.

Then Promit's company wanted to transfer him to Dubai. A higher position and better pay package. Promit had been excited. Besides it had been two years since he had moved to Calcutta and he was tired of the city. But Nita insisted they stay on. She was not keeping well, she said. For Promit it was a career boost and he did not want to miss out on the opportunity. So when Nita had gone for a regular check-up to her general physician's, he insisted she go to Dr Nandy for a specialised opinion. "Though there is nothing to worry about," he assured her. "Just a routine check up."

I really hope there is nothing wrong with Nita. Promit looked at his Rolex for the nth time. *Then why is it taking such a long time?* Promit could not help getting worried. *Shit. If Nita is not well, then my career will take a backseat. We will have to give Dubai a miss. Her folks will insist she stay here for treatment. I will not be able to manage the kids alone. And we will have to be holed up in this city for another couple of years. Amit Bhatia will get the transfer instead of me. Damn. Why of all times, did it have to be now? Couldn't she have held on for a few more months? Shit. I hope it is nothing serious...*

Nita lay in bed waiting...

"Sister, can you get the bed pan?" Nita feebly asked the nurse on day duty. She had just had a session of chemotherapy and she always felt weak after it. This was the third session in the past week and her blood count had dipped. She was groggy, nauseous and weak. Not to mention the pain. Sister Pearl from the local nurses bureau brought the pan and gently sat her up.

I wonder how much longer I will have to endure this? **Nita smiled at Sister Pearl.** *A year earlier she had been diagnosed with ovarian cancer. Of course, she was not told. But she knew from the hush hush tones of her relatives that something was amiss. She knew when, at thirty-four, she suddenly had to undergo a hysterectomy. The cancer has spread, she heard Sutapa telling one of her cousins over the phone one day. Then followed endless sessions of chemo and radiation at the Tata Hospital in Bombay. The best place for treatment, the doctors in Calcutta had assured the family. Her parents and sister as well as Promit had insisted that there was nothing to worry about. All would be well.*

If all was well, then why bring me to Tata? And why give me chemo and radiation? I am not a fool. I do have cancer. It came as a big shock to her. Why me, she cried silent tears for several days. When the tears were exhausted, she asked herself, how bad was her illness. And hoped desperately that she would be well someday. Soon.

I have to be. Atleast for Rumki and Jhumki's sake. Ten is a crucial age for girls and they will need their mother around for the next few years at least. God, just give me five-six years more. That is all I ask. I have to live for my parents. Ma is not keeping well. Her asthma is getting worse. At this age I cannot do this to her. And Sutapa. She will be so upset. My girls. My friends. My house. My clothes. My gold. Oh no. I will have to leave all that behind.

And Promit too. With his high-powered job, his friends, his social life, he is hardly likely to miss me. Will he be

a responsible parent in my absence? I doubt it. Inspite of my surgery, he took the Dubai posting. Even though everyone advised him against it. He explained that I will be better off here with my family and the children and that he needed to earn the extra money for my treatment. Said we could join him when I recover. But the question is, when will I recover?

Nita was waiting...

For Promit to return home. It was almost ten o'clock and he still had not returned. He had said there was some official dinner. Nita had tried to call but the cell phone was switched off. Unreachable, it had said. The children had gone to bed. And Nita was restless. She had settled his cupboard an hour back and discovered a lace kerchief. Two days back, when she and the children had just arrived in Dubai, she had found long, black strands of hair on the pillows on the master bed. It could not be Promit's. He did not have such long, jet-black hair. It had to be a woman's.

She was upset and reacted badly. "How could you sleep with another woman when I am dying," she cried showing him the long strand of hair. "Oh, shut up. That is yours," Promit had replied angrily.

"Mine? Mine?" she exclaimed, touching her bald pate. "From where?"

Promit was even more upset. "As it is I am going through financial and mental hell because of your illness and now you doubt my fidelity," he had shouted. She had never known this side of his. Promit was a changed man.

The children were frightened too. They had never seen their Baba so violent. He had almost hit her.

Yes, she realised. *He must be going through hell. The major surgery, the ongoing costs of chemo and radiation, the expensive medication to sustain her, the salaries of full-time nurses*—he did not spare any cost. She got the best of treatment. *I will take you to Sloane Kettering if need be, he had assured her.* **Nita smiled.** *He loves me after all. That is what marriage is all about. In sickness and in health....*

Of course I am better off with family and friends in Calcutta. And the children too are happier there with both sets of grandparents. Promit's parents have been such good guardians to Rumki and Jhumki. Then why am I upset?

Because he is staying apart? Alone? Or does he have company? Who knows? But he should, shouldn't he? Or what else is he to do? Sit and cry for me?

It is better this way. He has to earn a living too. Make money for me. If I have to survive. If I need to be taken to Sloane Kettering. Live to see Rumki and Jhumki marry. Wear my **dhakais** *and* **dhonekhalis**. *And the exquisite* **jadao** *set from Chandra Jewellers.*

No. It should not have been like this. Promit should not have come to Dubai. Leaving me and the kids. We would have managed. He should have been with me, holding my hand. Not the other woman's.

But then, how could he have helped. He is a man after all. Men and their hormones. And I have been ill for more than a year now. Unable to... satisfy his physical needs. But then what about the time before that. When he was unable to satisfy mine.... I did not go out of the house and seek... Never mind. There is nothing I can do now. Such is my fate...

Promit sat quietly, waiting...

"Hi baby," Mallika breezed in and threw him a kiss. "So? Been waiting for long?"

"Not really. About five minutes or so," Promit smiled.

"Oh. That is not much considering how much I have to wait for you," Mallika immediately regretted what she said. "Oh. I am sorry, honey," she touched his hand gently, "I did not mean it. I guess your wife's illness is just getting to me. That and my family's pressure to marry me off to that Tulu boy..." She paused, "I think it is affecting our relationship."

"That is okay," Promit said softly, "I understand. But I am helpless."

Nita was wasting away. The doctors had given up all hope. Not even Sloane Kettering as a last resort. The cancer had spread too far to control. And it was spreading faster every day. Galloping, they said. Soon it would eat into the vital organs. Promit could not bear to look at Nita.

Bald, emaciated, with bedsores and limp limbs. A living corpse.

The girls were going through hell too. Promit forbade them to see their mother. It would have been traumatic. They stayed with his parents. Thank God for them. Nita's father had just suffered a paralytic stroke. Between husband and daughter, her mother was totally shattered. Sutapa was a constant source of support. But then, how long could she hold out. Her sister's illness had taken a toll on her family life too.

And my life. I haven't a clue which way it is headed. Mallika is a lovely girl. Not nagging or demanding. Rumki and Jhumki are very fond of her too. But how long can she wait? Not indefinitely. There will be other men—unmarried, with no liabilities. Obviously more eligible. Will she leave me then? Or will she wait for me? If only fate intervened. If only....

Nita lay in bed waiting......

Weak. Helpless. Her entire body wracked with pain. Wasting away. But hoping...against all hopes.

Life is so cruel. I have nothing to look forward to. Baba just passed away. Ma is in a bad shape. My children have been kept away from me. Sutapa is suffering on my account. And Promit is waiting...waiting for me to die. So that he can marry Mallika. She must be praying too. In earnest.

For my death. It is two prayers against one. Do I still want to live? I don't know.
    This is not living. But I don't want to die....

Three months later...
    Promit was waiting...waiting for Nita to die.
    And Nita was waiting...waiting for a miracle.

ACKNOWLEDGEMENTS

No work can be a singular effort and likewise this book.

First of all I would like to thank Gulzar saab for coaxing me to wake up from my slumber and write. I am truly grateful to you.

To (M.F.) Husain saab for designing the cover.

To Khushwant Singh and Shobhaa De for giving me their time and valuable suggestions. Like the time when Khushwant pointed out that Sydney is spelt 'Sydney' and not 'Sidney'.

Mr. R.K. Mehra of Rupa for his encouragement and enthusiasm.

My editor, Atreyee Gohain, who has been with me from the very beginning. Deepthi Talwar at Rupa.

Joyda (Jayabrato Chatterjee) in Calcutta for suggestions here and there.

My friend, Dipa de Motwane for letting me go through the diaries of her great aunt Haimabati Ghosh on whose story I have based Indulata Debi's diaries.

To all my friends, who have provided me with inspiration for my stories.

To my husband, Om, who provided me with food and shelter whilst I wrote and hopefully will continue to do so while I continue to write. Also, for providing the first half of the title, 'Nine' of Nine On Nine. The latter half, 'On Nine' was mine. See what I mean by team work!

Especially to my staff (at home) without whom I would be tearing my hair. And most of all to my little son, Ishaan, at whom I have snapped often when I was busy writing. Ever forgiving and ever loving, Ishaan would look at me furiously typing away at the computer and say innocently, "Mama, you have a lovely handwriting"!